S0-BNF-394

"Agent Gallagher."

Alicia's soft voice stopped him on the upstairs landing of her ranch house. "Please, call me Leo," he said. "We're going to be in close quarters for a while."

She nodded but her eyebrows pinched together. "Leo. I appreciate what you're doing for us."

He nodded. "Keeping you and your family safe is my job, Alicia."

"And finding the man who wants your witness dead," she pointed out.

"Yes, that, too."

"I'll pray that you find him." Her words wrapped around him. The common bond of faith pleased him. He could use all the help he could get.

CLASSIFIED K-9 UNIT:
These lawmen solve the toughest cases with the help of their brave canine partners

Terri Reed's romance and romantic suspense novels have appeared on the *Publishers Weekly* top twenty-five and Nielsen BookScan's top one hundred lists, and have been featured in *USA TODAY*, *Christian Fiction Magazine* and *RT Book Reviews*. Her books have been finalists for the Romance Writers of America RITA® Award and the National Readers' Choice Award and finalists three times for the American Christian Fiction Writers Carol Award. Contact Terri at terrireed.com or PO Box 19555, Portland, OR 97224.

Books by Terri Reed

Love Inspired Suspense

Classified K-9 Unit

Guardian

Northern Border Patrol

Danger at the Border
Joint Investigation
Murder Under the Mistletoe
Ransom
Identity Unknown

Rookie K-9 Unit

Protect and Serve

Capitol K-9 Unit

Duty Bound Guardian

Visit the Author Profile page at Harlequin.com for more titles.

GUARDIAN

TERRI REED

 HARLEQUIN® LOVE INSPIRED® SUSPENSE

Special thanks and acknowledgment to Terri Reed for her participation in the Classified K-9 Unit miniseries.

Recycling programs for this product may not exist in your area.

LOVE INSPIRED BOOKS

ISBN-13: 978-0-373-45698-7

Guardian

Copyright © 2017 by Harlequin Books S.A.

www.Harlequin.com

Printed in U.S.A.

Deliver me, O Lord, from my enemies;
In You I take shelter.
—*Psalms* 143:9

Thank you to the editors at Love Inspired for the opportunity to work on this continuity. And a huge shout-out of gratitude for the brainstorming, encouragement and friendship to the other authors in this series: Laura Scott, Valerie Hansen, Lynette Eason, Shirlee McCoy and Lenora Worth.

PROLOGUE

The daylight broke over the horizon of the Los Angeles industrial district and muted morning light slashed through the high windows of the large two-floor warehouse. FBI agent Leo Gallagher pressed his back to the wall inside the cavernous structure's south entrance. The air was cool, but heavy with a mix of anticipation and vigilance.

His heart rate increased, not much, but enough that he took a calming breath. He tightened his hold on the leash of his canine partner, a chocolate Labrador named True.

The open floor plan of the bottom level was filled with containers and pallets that provided too many hiding places. That could be a problem. Shadows lurked above and in the recesses of the corners. No one said this job was easy. Far from it, and sweat beaded on his forehead behind his helmet.

Almost time? Leo glanced at fellow FBI agent Jake Morrow and his canine, a Belgian Malinois named Buddy.

Behind his tactical face guard, Jake nodded and signaled for Leo and True to proceed into the murky depths

of the purported hideout of the notorious Dupree syndicate, the criminal organization that the elite FBI Tactical
K-9 Unit had been working around the clock to bring
down for months.

But every time the team got close, the crime boss,
Reginald Dupree, and his uncle and second in command, Angus, managed to escape.

Not going to happen again. The first time could have
been coincidence, but after the second and third in-
stances, he knew something else was going on. That
was why Leo's boss had been tight-lipped about this
raid. No one outside the tight circle of the team knew
of today's operation in case there was a leak somewhere
in the Bureau.

The Tactical K-9 Unit was a special, classified branch
of the FBI that had settled in a nondescript building
in downtown Billings, Montana. The secret nature of
the team's cases needed anonymity to function. They
worked across the country, under the radar, to solve
tough crimes and deliver swift justice.

The thought of someone they knew and trusted
double-crossing them burned, and Leo hoped that
wasn't the case, but lives were at stake, either way. He
took a silent step. True stayed at his side.

Eerie silence scraped along Leo's nerves. The anonymous tip they'd received, sending the team to this location, had guaranteed them that Reginald and Angus
would be here. Plums ripe for the taking.

Across the expanse of open space, Leo saw fellow
team member Harper Prentiss, along with Star, her Ger-
man shepherd, and their boss, special agent in charge
Max West and his canine, a boxer by the name of Opal,

slip through another door and climb a staircase to the second floor.

A strange itch at the back of Leo's neck had him tensing. He'd been in this situation many times before, but this didn't feel right.

Glancing upward at the second-story balcony that rimmed the edges of the warehouse, he narrowed his gaze on the office doors. That itch worsened. Were Reginald and Angus Dupree up there? Waiting? Planning an ambush? If so, his team members would be in trouble.

Needing to provide his boss and fellow agent cover, Leo gestured to Jake. Morrow gave him the thumbs-up sign. In tandem they carefully moved farther into the warehouse, not wanting to draw attention to their presence.

True's ears perked up. The scruff of his neck rose. A deep growl emitted from his throat.

Breath stalling, Leo paused as he scanned the perimeter for whatever threat his partner sensed.

Then total pandemonium broke out.

Four men with automatic weapons appeared from around the sides of the two containers. A barrage of gunfire erupted. The deafening noise bounced off the walls.

Leo's heart revved into overdrive. Adrenaline surged. His pulse pounded in his ears as he dropped to one knee to return fire.

"Down!" Leo shouted to True. The dog dropped to his belly.

"Take cover!" Jake yelled.

Leo grabbed True's collar and tugged him behind a large container.

Something metal hit the concrete floor and a hissing

filled the air, followed by a cloudy haze. Leo gritted his teeth and fought past the stinging in his eyes and nose from the pepper-infused smoke sneaking beneath the face shield on his helmet.

The sound of a dog's yelp jolted through Leo. His heart slammed against his ribs. *True!* He quickly checked the dog's taut body for injury. None.

It had to be Buddy. Leo searched the gloom for Jake and his dog. He couldn't see either one. Had they retreated? Was Buddy hurt? Jake?

Leo flattened himself on the ground next to True, then tapped the canine on the flank. Together, they scuttled backward toward the door, keeping their heads down and out of the line of fire. A squad of Los Angeles police officers, dressed in tactical gear, filed past them.

With the arrival of backup, relief flooded through Leo.

Outside, he found Buddy lying on the ground, blood oozing from a wound in his hindquarters. Leo's stomach dropped. He knelt beside the dog, tore off his glove and used it as a compress against Buddy's injury. The dog whimpered.

"Where's Jake?" Leo rasped, wishing the dog could speak.

The whir of rotors close by had him jerking to his feet.

Buddy barked and, in a burst of energy, jumped up and took off, leading Leo and True around another building just as a black helicopter with no markings lifted from the ground. Buddy whined and continued to bark, his agitation clear as he sniffed a puddle of blood near where the helicopter had sat. Jake's blood?

A vise tightened around Leo's heart. He shaded his

eyes but couldn't see inside the tinted windows of the bird as it disappeared from view. This wasn't one of theirs. That meant...

"Gallagher!"

Leo turned to see his boss escorting Reginald Dupree from the warehouse while other officers brought out several of Dupree's henchmen.

Agent Harper Prentiss jogged over. "Angus Dupree escaped but we got Reginald." She tilted her head. "You okay?"

"No." His voice sounded ragged, the way he felt inside. He glanced at Buddy. The dog's distress tore at Leo. "Jake's been taken."

The team had captured the head honcho of the Dupree crime syndicate, but they'd lost a good agent in the process.

Guilt ate through Leo's gut like acid. He'd failed his team. He'd failed Jake. With fists clenched, Leo vowed he'd track down Angus Dupree and rescue his comrade, if it was the last thing he did on this earth.

ONE

"Mommy, where are the fishies?"

"Hey, be careful, buddy. Don't slip off the rock." Heart lurching, Alicia Duncan grabbed her son, Charlie, by the back of his green life vest. If he leaned over any farther, he would go headlong into Wyoming's Blackthorn River. His fishing pole clattered against the outcropping of smooth rocks, where they'd plopped down to fish. The exact place she'd fished from as a kid and teen. "Hang on to your pole, sweetie."

Heat bounced off the stones and reflected off the river water from the unseasonably warm April morning sun, making perspiration break out at her nape beneath her long dark hair. It was a beautiful spring day for spending time outdoors with her son in the middle of Wyoming's northwestern mountain range. The clear, smog-free air smelled sweet with the scent of ponderosa pines. So different from city life. A welcome change.

Alicia had always loved the river. About five miles downstream, the lazy flow of water cut a path through the rural town of Settler's Valley, where she'd grown up. There was something soothing, comforting even, about the way the mountain runoff filled the riverbed.

Especially in this particular area, where the river pooled into a deep canyon with high cliffs across the bank and more cliffs a little ways upstream. The water was deep enough here that she and her friends would jump off the cliffs into the river. Those had been the days when her husband had been her boyfriend and had promised her the world.

She sighed wistfully, as the bittersweet memories washed over her.

The summer after high school she'd married local football hero Jeff Duncan. She'd believed his promise. She'd believed him.

How innocent she'd been…

She and Jeff had escaped their small-town life for the city of Tacoma, Washington. He'd been her hero, both personally, as the love of her life and the father of her child, and professionally, as a highly decorated police officer. But nothing had been as it seemed.

Now eight years later, she was back home in Wyoming. A widow, raising her son and caring for her elderly father.

Oh, and let's not forget, licking her wounds. She hadn't even known until after the funeral that her marriage had been a sham. That Jeff hadn't been the man she thought he was.

Never again would she fall for charm and slick promises.

She shook her hands as if somehow the motion would relieve the restlessness that seemed to plague her these days.

"But I want to catch a fish," Charlie grumbled. Sunlight reflected off the water and lightened the blue of his eyes, shaped exactly like his father's. She could see

Jeff in the jut of Charlie's chin as well. Only on Charlie it looked good, not arrogant, the way it had on Jeff.

Okay, she was being uncharitable. There'd been a time when she'd loved her late husband. When he'd been everything to her. But that was before.

Alicia sighed and ruffled Charlie's thick dark hair, which he got from her gene pool. They'd been out fishing for over an hour without even a nibble. In the world of fishing, an hour was nothing, but with a three-year-old it was more than enough. So much for trout for dinner tonight. "I know, sweetie. They don't seem to be biting today."

She reeled in the lure on the fishing rod she'd borrowed from her father's collection. A fat worm still dangled from the hook. "How about we call it a day and treat ourselves to rainbow sherbet?"

"Yay! Sherbet." Charlie swung his legs in anticipation. His rubber boots slapped against the rock. She helped her little boy to his feet. He stood with his back to the water. She kept a hand on his shoulder in case he took a step backward.

The sound of a powerboat echoed off the walls of the stone cliffs rising up on the far side of the river. A boat, traveling downstream, rounded the bend into the mouth of the canyon. Alicia didn't pay the noise any attention as she gathered their fishing gear.

The motor sputtered to a halt. Silence echoed off the walls of stone. She glanced up to see a sleek, fiberglass sport boat floating in the middle of the river.

That was a little odd. The boat looked more like one used for waterskiing, not fishing.

A large man lifted a slim woman into his arms. Her head fell back, her long red hair cascaded in loose waves over the side of the boat and her arms hung limp at her sides. Was she asleep?

At this distance, about the length of a football field, Alicia couldn't tell. She frowned as her pulse sped up. What was he doing with the woman?

Without hesitation the man tossed the woman into the water. Her body splashed and then disappeared beneath the surface.

Alicia gasped and held her breath. Unwilling to believe what she'd just seen, she prayed the woman would come bursting to the surface. She didn't.

Shock punched Alicia in the stomach. She took a deep breath, and then another. She'd just witnessed a murder. Or rather, the woman was probably already dead and the man was disposing of her body.

A cold shiver of fear slithered down Alicia's spine. She glanced at Charlie, who studied a bug crawling on a nearby rock, and was grateful to realize he hadn't witnessed the horrifying scene.

When she returned her gaze to the boat, the killer shaded his eyes and locked his gaze on hers.

"Oh, no," Alicia breathed out in a panic.

The powerboat's engine roared to life, spurring Alicia into action. Her and Charlie's only chance was to get to the shelter of the forest along the riverbank and make their way to the marina, about a half mile away. She knew this part of the river like the back of her hand. She and her school friends had spent almost every summer day along the shores of the Blackthorn River.

"Charlie, we need to go," she urged. "Now."

"Why, Mommy?"

This was one time she couldn't explain her rationale. She hated when parents of the kids she taught gave their kids commands without explaining the reasons why the child needed to comply. "Because I said so" wasn't an acceptable form of communication in Alicia's book.

But right now she didn't have the mental or emotional wherewithal to use her words, let alone explain that she'd just witnessed a man dump a woman into the river and now said man was coming after them. She needed Charlie to do as she asked. "Charlie, please, do as I ask. Get up."

She glanced over her shoulder. The sport boat was closing the distance. Was that a gun the man held in his hand?

Terror fastened around her throat like a noose. *Please, Lord, protect us!*

She hooked her hobo bag with one hand, slipped the strap over her shoulder to hang across her body and grabbed Charlie around the waist with her other arm and drew him to her chest, using her own body as a shield against the man with the gun.

"Mommy!" Charlie protested. "Too tight."

"Sorry, honey," she muttered but didn't lessen her hold as she stepped carefully off the rock, leaving behind the fishing gear. Dad would be irritated, but she didn't have the time to grab the poles and tackle box. She'd have to come back later, when it was safe.

She slipped slightly in the soft dirt along the shore, but the bottoms of her boots dug in and kept her upright. She was thankful she'd worn her hiking boats instead of the deck shoes she'd almost put on this morning. With the roar of the powerboat drawing closer, she ran into the woods and headed south. There wasn't a clear trail, but she didn't hesitate. She knew her way around these woods and just hoped whoever was on the boat didn't.

The sudden quiet sent a fresh swell of terror hurtling through her. Had the man reached the shore? Behind her, something crashed through the forest. A loud pop and a thud in the tree to her right startled her. Debris spit from the tree trunk. The killer was shooting at them!

Using every ounce of strength she possessed, she forced her legs to pump faster. She zigzagged through the trees and scrub brush. Jeff had always said a moving target was harder to hit, especially an erratic one.

"Hang on to me, Charlie," she said softly as she hunkered down, trying to make them as small a target as possible.

She broke through the trees to the marina's gravel parking lot. She ran down the parking lane, intending to head straight to the boathouse for help. But her car was right there. The forceful thought to get away, to put as much distance between her and the killer, pounded inside her head.

She jammed her hand into her hobo bag, and her fingers curled around her key fob. She pressed the button that unlocked the doors and ducked behind a car parked two spaces from her own white all-wheel-drive hatchback. She needed to catch her breath. To think.

Charlie's hands grasped her face. "Scared, Mommy."

"Yes, I know, sweetie. A bad man is after us." Staring into her son's trusting gaze, Alicia vowed she'd do whatever it took to keep her son safe. "So I need you to be very quiet, okay?"

The skidding of feet on the gravel echoed through the still air. The killer had reached the parking lot. She shuddered with dread.

Please, let him think we went to the boathouse, Alicia prayed.

She scooted closer to the car so that her feet were blocked by the tires in case he looked beneath the undercarriages of the row of vehicles hoping to pinpoint where they were. Terror ricocheted through her and she held her breath. As if sensing her fear, Charlie buried his face in the side of her neck and grabbed fistfuls of her shirt.

Listening intently, she made out the crunch of heavy steps on the loose rock as the killer moved closer. She tilted her head and closed her eyes. He was coming down the lane to her right. Adjusting her grip on Charlie, she edged to the left and around the back of the vehicle.

In a low crouch, she risked sprinting to the rear end of the next vehicle. She pressed her back to the tailgate of a truck and waited. After a moment, she darted to her car. Carefully, she opened the back passenger door far enough for her and Charlie to climb inside.

Pulling the door closed but not latching it for fear the click would alert the killer, she squatted awkwardly on the floor and set Charlie on the seat. She quickly undid his life vest and set it aside. "Charlie, I need you to get into your seat and buckle up, okay?"

He nodded solemnly, his eyes big and his lower lip quivering. She hated scaring him like this, but there was nothing to be done. They needed to get away.

She stayed crouched behind the driver's seat until he was secured in his car seat. She grabbed the life vest and pressed it to his chest. "Hold on to this, okay?"

It wouldn't stop a bullet but she had nothing else to provide a barrier.

Taking a deep breath, she squeezed herself across the middle console and climbed into the driver's seat. She slunk down in the seat and could barely see over the dashboard. Adrenaline surged as she saw the back of the killer's head as he lumbered toward the boathouse. She hesitated with her hand on the key in the ignition. The second she fired up the engine, he'd know where they were.

When the killer reached the boathouse and disappeared inside, she sprang into action. She started the car, threw the gearshift into Reverse and stepped on the gas. Heart in her throat, she barely managed to brake before hitting the car parked in the opposite space. She spun the wheel, put the vehicle into Drive and stomped her foot on the gas pedal. The car tires spun and found traction, and they hurtled forward.

The killer ran out of the boathouse with the gun aimed at the car. Alicia sucked in a quick breath and took a sharp turn at the end of the lane. She sped toward the main road, which would take her into town and to the police station.

Up ahead one of the three traffic lights turned red. She took her foot off the gas, letting the car slow, and glanced in the rearview mirror. A big 4x4 truck barreled out of the marina parking lot and raced toward her.

Her breath hitched. She looked in both directions for oncoming traffic. Seeing that it was safe, she gunned the accelerator. The car shot forward through the intersection. She hung a quick right on Elm Street, then a sharp left on Cedar Drive, hoping that the killer wouldn't be able to track her. Racing down Cedar, she hooked another right on Evergreen Avenue. Up ahead the new brick building of Settler's Valley police station was a beacon of sanctuary.

The squeal of tires behind her sent a chill of terror

over her flesh. The killer's truck rounded the corner and roared down the street after her. She gripped the steering wheel so tight that her hands ached.

Only a few more feet to safety. She laid her hand on the horn in an effort to attract attention. She lifted a prayer to God that someone inside the building would hear the commotion and come out to investigate.

Because surely, the killer wouldn't risk doing something to her and Charlie within plain sight of the police station, would he?

Leo and True slipped through the ground-floor doors of the FBI's Tactical K-9 Unit headquarters in Billings, Montana.

His boss, Max West, had called for a team meeting, pulling Leo and True in from a morning run. His T-shirt was damp with sweat and his running shoes were silent on the concrete floor. He hoped this powwow meant some news about Jake.

Leo left True in the care of one of the dog trainers, then scrubbed a hand over his bristled jaw as he took the stairs. He'd hardly slept in the week since Jake went missing. They'd had no word on his whereabouts. The silence and lack of information concerned him deeply. For the millionth time, Leo prayed that his buddy was alive and that the team would find him.

The six-story brick building was the unit's base of operations, but at any moment each team member could be deployed to any crime scene in any state in the country. That was how they'd ended up in that Los Angeles warehouse a week ago.

The K-9 unit consisted of the training facility on the ground floor, while the second floor housed the agents' offices and computer tech center. The other floors were occupied by a variety of government officials. Both the training center and the presence of other governmental employees helped to disguise the team's covert operations.

Stopping by his desk in the bull pen, Leo shrugged off his lightweight jacket and hung it over the back of his desk chair. He checked for messages in his inbox on his FBI-issued laptop, flagged a couple to return to later, then headed to the communications center. Pausing in the doorway, he noticed the team wasn't gathered there. There was only Dylan O'Leary, the computer genius. "Hey."

Dylan spun from the bank of computer monitors to grin at him. His spiky, sandy-blond hair and dark-framed glasses screamed techno geek while his loud Hawaiian shirt over his official FBI Tactical K-9 Unit polo made it clear he was a man with a sense of humor. "How's it going, Leo?"

"Going." Leo leaned a shoulder against the door-jamb. "You?"

Dylan sighed and rubbed a hand over the back of his neck. "I miss Zara, but Radar and I are doing okay. We're getting along."

Leo was glad to hear his fiancée's dog wasn't giving him trouble. Zara was at Quantico, training to be an official FBI agent so that she could come back and officially join the team. "Where is everyone?"

"The debriefing room."

Leo chuckled. In other words, the kitchen. "You coming?"

Dylan turned back to his computer monitors. "I'll be there in a minute."

Leo left Dylan to his gadgets and headed into the large open area of the "debriefing" space. Along the far wall was a state-of-the-art kitchen, complete with oven, stovetop and fridge, all in stainless steel. A bank of windows provided natural light and an extra-large monitor hung on the wall near the door.

A long hand-carved wooden table with bench seats dominated the middle of the room. The team was already seated and munching on fruit platters and trays of pastries from Petrov Bakery, a favorite with all the agents.

Max stood at the coffee machine, making himself a latte. He glanced up and tipped his chin at Leo. He was a tall man with short blond hair and a ragged scar on one side of his face. "The gang's all here."

Not quite. Jake was missing.

The familiar burn of guilt ate at Leo, killing any appetite he might have had. He straddled the end of the closest bench next to Ian Slade. The tall, muscular agent cracked a joke that had Harper Prentiss and Julianne Martinez and the team's general assistant, Christy Burton, laughing. As usual, the good-humored Ian was charming the ladies.

Max moved to the head of the table and sat. "Where are we with the Dupree case?"

"Reginald Dupree isn't talking," Harper replied. "He's lawyered up and so have his henchmen. The US district attorney is spitting mad about it."

"Angus Dupree escaped—we assume on the helicopter," Timothy Ramsey, a junior agent, added. He sat across the table from Leo between Harper and another junior agent, Nina Atkins.

"And Agent Morrow?" Max asked, his piercing blue

eyes surveying his team. "Jake's brother, Zeke, has been hounding me for answers. I don't have any to give yet."

Leo's jaw tightened. It had to be tough for Zeke, thinking he'd never see his brother again. Jake had mentioned once he and his brother weren't close and barely spoke, but still… Family was family.

"The press is also pestering me for a statement," Christy said with a flip of her auburn hair. "I can't keep them in the dark for much longer."

"It's been a week and no word," Julianne said, her voice soft. No doubt she was thinking Jake was dead. Leo wouldn't accept that.

"Angus took Jake," Leo stated. "We know that. We tested the blood we found at the scene. It was Jake's."

Ian swiveled toward Leo. "Why would they take him?"

"For leverage. To get information out of him." Leo couldn't help the growl in his voice. He should have had Jake's and Buddy's backs.

"Angus might use Jake to reduce Reginald's sentence," Harper added.

Ian shook his head, his normal good humor disappearing as he sobered. "If Angus was going to use him, he'd have done so by now, right?"

"Jake has intimate knowledge of our investigation into the Duprees," Harper said. "He knows that we have Esme Dupree stashed away in witness protection, ready to testify against her brother."

"But Jake doesn't have access to Esme's whereabouts," Ian pointed out.

Dylan stepped into the room carrying a computer device. "Hey, guys, I received an alert on a crime I think you might want to hear about." He tapped some keys on his console. "A witness in Settler's Valley, Wyoming, claims to have seen a man dumping a body into the Blackthorn River. By the description, it sounds like the victim could be Esme Dupree."

Leo's stomach muscles clenched. Could the report from Wyoming be true? Had a witness seen Esme Dupree's dead body? Without Esme, their case would fall apart. "Is the witness reliable?"

"The Settler's Valley police chief thinks so," Dylan replied. "A schoolteacher named Alicia Duncan. She saw the killer, who she claims shot at her and her three-year-old son."

Leo's breath caught in his throat. A child. Memories assaulted him. He fought them back with the practice of over two decades. He focused his gaze on his boss. "We'll go. True is the only dog qualified for the task." True's specialty was Water Search and Detection.

Max's eyebrows hitched upward. "Good point. Leo, you and True make your way to Wyoming. I'll call the US Marshals to verify they haven't lost our witness. Dylan, contact the nearest SAR team that has a qualified diver and send them to Settler's Valley. Also get everything you can about this new witness to Leo, as well as any info you can get on the supposed killer."

"On it." Dylan pivoted and exited as quickly as he'd arrived.

By the time Leo had showered and changed into khakis and a black, long-sleeve polo shirt with the FBI logo on the breast pocket, Dylan had a dossier on Alicia Duncan ready.

After he had True secured in his special compartment of the official K-9 unit SUV, he flipped through the file on the witness, getting the basics. She seemed legit. A widowed schoolteacher with a young child living with her father. Not some attention-seeking nutcase wasting his time. Leo placed the folder on the passenger seat and set off for Settler's Valley, Wyoming. He'd interview the witness and then take True to the river. If there was truly a body to be found, True would find the victim. He always did.

TWO

"Mommy, I'm hungry," Charlie whined. "I want sherbet."

"Me, too, honey." Stomach cramping with hunger, Alicia smoothed back Charlie's dark hair as he bent over the coloring book one of the female officers had scrounged up along with a box of crayons. Three hours had passed since she'd come blazing through the police station doors with Charlie in her arms.

The police chief, Dwayne Jarrett, was a friend of her father's and had escorted her to his office, where he listened to her nearly hysterical account of what she'd seen and that the killer was after her and Charlie.

She wasn't sure Dwayne had believed her until he'd gone outside to move her car off the lawn, where she'd left it parked near the front entrance, and seen the bullet hole in the back bumper. After that he'd taken her seriously. Like her word hadn't been enough.

She sighed with frustration and glanced out the office window. The bull pen was filled with officers busy doing whatever they did. She'd spied a vending machine on the way in. Tired of waiting, she decided to take action. "How about we go see if we can find something to eat or drink."

Hitching her bag over her shoulder, she rose and held out her hand to Charlie. He set aside his crayon and clasped her hand. His tiny fingers curled through hers and love for this little precious gift from God exploded in her chest. She had many regrets about her marriage, but Charlie wasn't one of them.

She opened the office door, and they slipped out into the hall. She bought raisins and apple juice from the vending machine then ducked into the restroom. After freshening up, they returned to the chief's office. She'd expected it to be empty, so she was a bit discombobulated to find the chief sitting behind his desk and another man taking up a good portion of the small space.

He had short blond hair and wide shoulders beneath a jacket with the acronym of the Federal Bureau of Investigation on the back. What was the FBI doing here?

Chief Jarrett leaned to the side to see her around the other man. "There you are."

The federal agent turned. Alicia sucked in a sharp breath. The man had the greenest eyes she'd ever seen, and they assessed her from head to toe with an inscrutable expression that made her want to fiddle with her hair. She straightened to her full height of five-ten. She was so done with being intimidated by men, especially law-enforcement types.

Next to the agent sat a handsome chocolate-colored Labrador attached to a leash held loosely in the agent's hand. The dog tilted his head at them as if he, too, was assessing her and Charlie.

"Doggy!" Charlie pulled on her hand, trying to escape from her grasp, but she held on tight, not sure how good an idea it would be for her son to launch himself at a K-9 dog.

"No, sweetie. The dog is working."

The agent's eyes flared with obvious surprise, and then an appreciative gleam shone through the sharp emerald-colored gaze. "It's okay. True won't bite him."

"*True.* That's an interesting name," Alicia murmured, still reluctant to release Charlie's hand. "We'll not bother the dog."

Jarrett gestured to the fed. "Agent Leo Gallagher is with an elite K-9 investigation team for the Bureau. He would like to ask you some questions."

A gentle smile curved the corners of Agent Gallagher's mouth and her heart did a funny little move she'd never experienced before. What was that about?

"Ms. Duncan, please have a seat." He flicked his hand toward the place she and Charlie had recently vacated.

Staunchly ignoring her inner reaction, she lifted her chin. "I'll stand, thank you."

She settled Charlie back in the chair and opened the goodies for him to munch on. Though his attention was clearly on the dog, she remained a barrier between them. Despite the agent's assurance that his canine wouldn't bite, she refused to risk it.

Aware that she was making the agent wait, she took a bracing breath before turning her attention back to the blond-haired fed. "I've already told the chief everything I can remember."

Agent Gallagher held her gaze. "Yes, he's shared your statement with me. I would like to hear it for myself."

Her eyes darted to the chief. "I'd prefer not to explain in front of my son."

Charlie didn't need to hear the details now or ever. When she'd first arrived a female officer had taken Charlie aside for the few moments it had taken Alicia to explain to the chief what had happened.

Jarrett stood. "Alicia, Agent Gallagher will be taking the lead on this case. Come on, Charlie. Let's take a walk."

Alicia bit her bottom lip to keep from protesting. She didn't like having Charlie out of her sight. But she could hardly protest given that the chief would protect her son. Not only because it was his job, but also because they were a close-knit community. The folks of Settler's Valley took care of one another. The adage that it took a village was true for this small town.

After her mother's death, the citizens had rallied around her father and made sure he'd had everything he needed. Alicia regretted she hadn't been here at the time. But she was now, and she had every intention of making up for lost time.

When the chief and Charlie were gone, the agent hitched a hip on the edge of the desk. "Now, start from the beginning."

The dog took his cue from his handler and lay down with his head on his paws.

"Fine." Though the two officers might be relaxed, an anxious quiver ran through her. She fought to keep her voice even as she described what she'd witnessed on the river, the killer chasing after her and Charlie, the gunshots assailing them, and finally ending up at the police station.

The agent's stoic expression never wavered. "The truck was reported stolen from the marina a half hour ago."

"That makes sense," she said. "He'd come from up-river."

"If you sat with a forensic artist, would you be able to give a detailed description of the suspect?"

Acid churned in her tummy as she recalled the man's face. "Oh, yes. I doubt I'll forget his image anytime soon." She shuddered. "Dark, cold eyes. He had a shaved head. Not tall, but bulky."

"I'll send for an artist. Did your son see the man as well?"

"No, thankfully."

"That's a blessing," the agent murmured.

Was this man a believer or was he using the word as a nicety as some people did? "It is a blessing from God. A huge one."

Something flickered in his eyes before his expression turned all-business again. "The woman you saw go into the water… Did you get a look at her face?"

"No. I only saw her long red hair and her limp body." She shivered at the horrible memory.

"Would you be able to pinpoint where the body went into the water?"

"Of course, Agent Gallagher. I'm surprised the police haven't already gone out to drag the river."

"Call me Leo. Settler's Valley isn't necessarily equipped for that. A diver is on his way from Sheridan. I'd like you to go with us to the scene of the crime. My partner and I will find the body so the diver can bring her up. True's a trained water-search dog."

Doubt made her voice quiver. "But it's been hours. The woman is at the bottom of the river. It's deep in the canyon."

"The woman's body will give off gases and liquids that True will pick up."

She swallowed back the bile rising up. This was one of the many ugly sides of police work. "I can't leave Charlie."

"He seems to be in good hands with the chief."

"Wouldn't the chief want to be at the river when they bring up the victim?"

He arched an eyebrow. "You heard the chief—I'm taking the lead on this case."

Not liking his superior tone, she lifted her chin. "Why? What does a small-town murder have to do with the feds?"

He pressed his lips together and a muscle ticked in his jaw. "I can't divulge the details of the case, Ms. Duncan." He held open the door. "Shall we?"

She hated being left in the dark. Irritation spread through her chest. She preceded the agent out of the office, determined to get this over with so she and her son could resume their quiet life without murder, mayhem and too-handsome federal agents with secrets to muddy the waters.

Leo brought his vehicle to a halt in the gravel parking lot behind the Blackthorn River marina. He glanced at the woman beside him as she stared straight ahead in stony silence. Alicia Duncan had a nice profile, a straight nose, with high cheekbones. Her long, wavy dark hair hung over her slim shoulders. She wore a light pink tank top and jean capris with hiking boots. Very earthy.

Nothing like any of the schoolteachers he'd had as a kid. From the dossier he'd read, he knew she'd grown up in Settler's Valley but had lived in Tacoma, Washington, for the better part of a decade.

She popped open the passenger door, but before she could step out, he laid a hand on her arm. "Wait for me and True."

She met his gaze and blinked, the pupils of her bright blue eyes a bit too large, indicating she hadn't fully recovered from her earlier ordeal. Leo would imagine the pretty single mom had never been shot at before, nor ever had to run for her life.

Leo hated that she and her son had had to witness such evil and be put in danger. But while he was on the case, he wouldn't let anything happen to them.

He gave her arm what he hoped would be a reassuring pat before he climbed out of his SUV and released True from the compartment in the back. The Lab sniffed the air, his tail stiffening, his ears forward and his mouth closed—all signs that he was detecting something of interest to him, but not yet a threat.

No doubt he could smell or hear the rushing of the river, which told him they were about to go to work.

Leo walked around to the passenger side and opened Alicia's door. She gave him a tight smile as she slipped out of the vehicle. A police cruiser parked beside them and two officers stepped out.

"I'm Officer Jenkins and this is Officer Reynolds," the older of the two officers said, introducing himself and his partner. "The chief said we're to stick close to Ms. Duncan."

Leo nodded and shook the men's hands. "Much appreciated."

Alicia hung back with her arms down at her sides,

but there was no mistaking the tension pinching the corners of her mouth.

They didn't have to wait long before a white truck with the Sheridan police department logo on the side turned into the parking lot. It was towing an aluminum flat-bow boat sporting an electric trolling motor to allow them to move slowly through the water while True searched the surface for scents.

The driver pulled next to their vehicles and rolled down his window. He had a craggy face that had spent a lot of time in the sun. Dark eyes regarded them beneath black winged brows. He wore a cowboy hat pulled low over his ears. "Agent Gallagher?"

Leo stepped over. "I'm Gallagher. You're Craig Sampson?"

"Yep, that's me." His gaze shifted to True. "He's a handsome fellow."

"Thanks."

"I'll put in and then you and your dog can come aboard."

"My witness will show us where she saw the body go in."

Craig glanced over at Alicia. "I don't have room for the pretty lady and the officers."

"They'll stay on land. She was upriver fishing from shore, so she'll lead the officers through the woods to the spot."

"Sounds like a plan." Craig rolled up the window and drove to the ramp, where he made a wide arc and then backed the boat into the water.

Leo turned to Alicia and the officers. "Ms. Duncan, I'll need you to lead Officers Jenkins and Reynolds to where you and Charlie were fishing. We'll head upstream with our diver and meet you there."

"I can do that," she said. She squared her shoulders. "This way, gentlemen."

She strode away, forcing the two officers to hustle to keep up. Leo couldn't stop the slight smile curving his lips. The woman may have been rattled and afraid earlier, but she was doing a bang-up job of pushing through to get the job done. He admired grit like that.

True started after Alicia. Leo whistled, bringing the dog to heel. "We're taking to the water, boy." He grabbed the necessary equipment from the back of the SUV and they headed to the boat ramp.

Once they were settled in the boat, True took his position standing at the bow, his official FBI K-9 life vest around his torso and Leo, with matching life vest, sitting on the middle transom. Craig fired up the boat. He'd pulled on a dry dive suit that covered him from head to toe, leaving only an oval for his face.

They puttered away from the marina and headed upstream. Anticipation and dread twisted in Leo's chest. He didn't want the body to be Esme Dupree. She'd witnessed her brother murdering one of his associates and had agreed to testify against him. And since the other Dupree sister, Violetta, who was clean as far as they could discover, had refused to cooperate, the FBI's case against Reginald Dupree hinged on Esme's testimony.

But whoever the poor woman was at the bottom of the river, her loved ones deserved justice for her murder.

They rounded a bend in the river, where the landscape on the right side of the river changed abruptly from wooded terrain to towering cliffs of sediment and stone. On the left side, the woods thinned and gave way to boulders that gradually rose to another steep cliff.

Leo shaded his eyes and scanned the shore, immediately spotting Alicia and the two officers standing on a smooth outcropping of rocks.

"Head over there," Leo instructed Craig.

When they were within shouting distance of the rocks, Leo noticed fishing poles and a tackle box. This must have been where Alicia and her son had been when they'd seen the killer.

Alicia pointed upstream and yelled, "He came from that direction and stopped about three hundred and sixty feet straight out from here." She gestured to the rocks beneath her feet.

"That's helpful and gives us a place to start." Leo stared, admiring the pretty lady. Her hair lifted slightly in the wind that had kicked up. Sunlight reflected in her piercing blue eyes. "You and the officers can head back to the station." He didn't want her here to see the body when they found the victim.

Alicia shook her head. "I want to make sure she's found. Someone has to stand up for her."

Respecting her decision, he saluted her then turned to Craig. "You heard the lady."

Craig slowly turned the boat toward the middle of the river. True stood on the bow, his head up, gaze alert. Leo tuned in to the dog's nuances the farther away from shore they traveled. He documented the time and distance from land on the notepad he carried. They circled the area where Alicia had pointed. True showed no signs of alerting.

"Head downstream," Leo instructed Craig.

Since the body hadn't been weighted down, it most

likely had been swept along by the river's current. Craig zigzagged the boat from one shore to the other, moving farther and farther away from the spot. Leo wondered if maybe the suspect had come back and removed the woman's body. Frustration curled in his stomach.

Then True shifted. He licked his lips and shuffled his paws, clear signs he was picking up a scent. Leo's pulse jumped. The dog's tail went down as he craned his neck, dipping his nose toward the water. He pivoted, and then leaned over the starboard side. Keeping his snout at the surface of the water, True walked the length of the boat and stepped easily over the bench seat.

Anticipation revving through him, Leo gestured for Craig to make a slow turn. True retraced his steps, barking an alert. He scratched and nipped at the water. Knowing the animal had scent glands in the roof of his mouth, Leo interpreted these actions as the sign this was the spot.

"Good boy." Leo grasped True's life vest to keep the dog from jumping in.

Leo nodded at Craig, who shut off the motor, then strapped on a buoyance compensator, his mask and oxygen tank. The man sat on the side of the boat and fell backward into the water. True barked and lunged for the water. Leo continued to hold him back.

"No, boy," Leo said, adjusting his grip on True. "We're staying here."

Leo and True both watched the surface of the river. Leo pulled on latex gloves in anticipation of handling the body and prepared the large, waterproof plastic body bag. His gaze darted back to the shore, where Alicia stood sentinel on the rocks, flanked by the two officers. She held her head up and her shoulders back like a fierce warrior. She was tall and so very appealing. He admired her commitment to being a voice for the victim. Most people would want to bail the second they could. Not Alicia. He liked that about her.

Bubbles rose as Craig broke through the surface. In his arms he held a red-haired woman. Anxiety curled through Leo. He gave True the command to lie down so he could help Craig bring the woman's inert body onto the boat and into the body bag. Smoothing back a chunk of matted hair, Leo inhaled sharply then let out his breath in a *swoosh*.

It wasn't Esme. They still had their prime witness in the Dupree case. But there was enough of a resemblance that for a moment he'd thought the worst. And though Esme was still alive, sorrow welled within him because this woman wasn't.

Now he had the difficult task of identifying the victim and informing the family.

He took his cell phone from his pocket and called Chief Jarrett, who promised to send the coroner to meet them at the marina. The coroner would take possession of the body and then call in a forensic pathologist to do an autopsy.

Leo then called headquarters. The team's general assistant immediately answered. "FBI Tactical K-9 Unit, Christy Burton speaking."

"It's Leo. Is Max available?"

"Good afternoon, Leo. He's on another line talking to the US Marshals. Is this urgent or can he call you back?"

There wasn't much Max could do from headquarters, so not urgent. "Tell him to call me. I found what we were looking for."

"I'll tell him." Christy signed off and Leo tucked his phone back in his pocket.

Before he could zip the bag closed, Craig murmured, "There's something pinned to her clothes."

A baggie had indeed been pinned to the collar of her shirt. Leo had missed it at first because of her hair. And inside the baggie was a note, the words clearly visible through the plastic.

It's not sisterly to snitch, Esme.

THREE

Alicia stood on the outcropping of rocks, her heart pounding so hard she thought it might burst from her chest. This spot held so many fun and cherished memories, but now…

Out on the river, Leo and the diver had pulled the victim from the water. Averting her gaze, Alicia sent up a prayer for the woman's family. They would need God's peace and comfort when they learned of their loved one's demise. She hoped justice would be served. For both this woman's sake, as well as for Alicia and Charlie's safety. She couldn't forget the man who'd done this, the one who'd shot at and chased after them and was still out there.

The boat carrying Leo, the diver and True motored downstream. Alicia watched them for a moment. Thoughts raced through her head. A feeling of uncertainty flowed through her.

Agent Gallagher glanced back and waved. She automatically raised her hand in response, signaling what, she wasn't sure. See you later? A job well done?

They'd found the victim and would be able to give the woman's family closure. That had to be worth something in the grand scheme of things. It hurt Alicia's heart that anyone should have to die at the hands of another.

Her thoughts turned to her late husband, Jeff. Had he realized in those moments after being shot while on duty that he was leaving this world? Had he found himself regretting the less honorable things in his life? Of the sweet little boy they'd made together, Charlie? Had he thought of her?

She closed her eyes and willed the hurt and pain to dissipate.

"We should meet Agent Gallagher at the marina," Officer Jenkins said in a gentle tone, forcing her to focus on the here and now.

"Will you grab the tackle box?" Alicia picked up her and Charlie's fishing poles. She had half expected them to be gone, taken by someone either hoping to add to their own collection, or who would turn them into the marina's lost and found. Lots of people used the rocks to fish, but apparently not today.

A part of her wished she and Charlie hadn't been there. She couldn't quiet the unease inside her, but if that had been the case, no one would have known about the woman. Sighing, she knew she would have to trust God that she was where she was supposed to be today. He'd seen her through so much. She couldn't forget that now.

Ever so slowly, she and the two officers made their way through the trees and underbrush. She stopped by the tree where the killer's bullet had taken out a chunk of the bark and shivered. Pointing at the hole, she said, "The killer shot at us here."

Officer Reynolds took a picture of the hole in the

tree with his phone. He did some pointing of his own. "See these gouges?"

She nodded.

"The assailant must have come back and dug out the bullet," he observed. "But we have the one from your car, which unfortunately didn't yield any clue to the suspect's identity."

They continued onward.

A careful killer. Would he see her as a detail to be eliminated?

Fear scratched at her mind, making her stumble over a root in the ground. She had to stay focused. The last thing she needed was to twist an ankle or worse.

She sent up a grateful prayer that Charlie hadn't seen the man. However, the killer couldn't know that. She hoped, prayed, the man wouldn't consider Charlie a threat. A three-year-old wouldn't make for a reliable witness.

Alicia led the way toward the gravel parking lot. They were only a few feet from clearing the forest when a noise sounded to the right that made the hairs on her arms rise. She darted behind a tree, trying to make herself as invisible as possible.

Officer Jenkins withdrew his sidearm. "It could be anything. A bear or an elk."

Or a killer tracking her movements.

Paranoid much? The killer wouldn't risk capture by sticking around, would he?

"Let's hustle," Officer Reynolds advised as he cupped her elbow and increased their pace.

They broke through the forest onto the gravel lot. With the two officers flanked on either side of her, they made their way to the marina at a fast clip.

The county coroner was already at the boat launch as the boat carrying Leo, True, the diver and the corpse arrived. Alicia and her escorts hung back as the body was loaded into the back of the coroner's van. Both officers were twitchy, their sharp-eyed gazes returning to the woods as if they expected something or someone to come barreling out of the forest.

Alicia kept the agent's SUV between her and the edge of the forest as a shield, just in case. She was all Charlie had left. He and her father needed her in one piece and breathing.

Leo shook hands with the diver and then, with True at his heels, he walked toward Alicia. There was a grimness to the set of his mouth and a tension in his wide shoulders that hadn't been there before he'd gone out on the river.

"Thank you, Ms. Duncan, for your help today," he said. "Having you point out the victim's body's location saved us time. I'm hopeful the forensics will lead us to her killer."

"I pray so," she murmured. "That man can't be allowed to get away with this crime."

Leo's green eyes darkened. "He won't."

There was a world of determination and conviction in his husky tone that made Alicia suspect Agent Leo Gallagher was the type of man who never quit once he was on a case. For the victim's sake, she appreciated that trait in the man.

Jenkins caught Leo's attention. "Sir, can I talk to you a moment?"

Leo nodded and the two men stepped away, but not far enough that she couldn't hear the officer telling Leo about the scare they'd had in the woods. Alicia wasn't sure why the officer felt the need to leave her out of the conversation. She'd been there, too. She'd heard the unsettling noise. She just wanted to go back to the police station, grab Charlie and head home to the ranch.

Leo shook hands with Jenkins and Reynolds before they climbed into their cruiser.

"Let's get you to your son," Leo said as he held open the passenger door of his SUV.

Grateful to him for understanding her unspoken desire to return to Charlie, she whispered, "Thank you. I worry."

"Of course you do. That's what moms are supposed to do, right?"

Something in his tone caught her attention as she climbed into the passenger seat. While Leo and True took their places in the SUV, she struggled to reason out the note of…not sarcasm but resentment, maybe. Hmm. It was subtle but there. She'd learned to hear the subtext in words and voices as a teacher. Doing so had helped her detect a case of child abuse at her last school.

However, she curbed her curiosity about Agent Gallagher. Whatever his issues were, they were his and she had no desire to get roped into any type of relationship with the man, even if only one of sympathy. In less than an hour she'd be on her way home, and Leo would no longer be in her life.

"What did you hear in the woods?" he asked, surprising her.

She shrugged, hoping to come across as nonchalant. "Movement. But it could have been any number of things. The forests are home to many different animals both large and small."

He slanted her a quick glance then returned his gaze to the road. "You weren't alarmed?"

Her mouth twisted in a wry smile. "I didn't say that. After what I witnessed today, being a bit jumpy is understandable."

"Yes, it is understandable. I have to say you're handling everything remarkably well."

"Thanks. My late husband was a cop. I think maybe that has something to do with it."

"My condolences on your husband's death. From the sounds of it, he was a hero."

She arched her eyebrows and ignored the comment about her husband being a hero. For Charlie's sake, she wouldn't ever dispute the assumption. She wanted him to be proud of his father. She hoped her son never learned the truth about the kind of man Jeff had truly been. "From the sounds of it? Did you do a background check on me?"

"I wouldn't be a very good investigator if I didn't do my homework," Leo replied evenly.

"Right. Of course." She shouldn't be surprised. For all he knew, she could be a nutcase wanting attention by claiming to have witnessed a murder.

Still, it made her feel vulnerable to know he had information about her that she hadn't shared with him. Was there a file on her? What did it say? Was her and Jeff's dirty laundry listed in the file? She shuddered as she did anytime she thought about Jeff's cheating and lying.

They arrived at the police station, and Alicia didn't wait for Leo and True, but jumped out the second the SUV halted and hurried inside. She found Charlie with the chief's wife, Lynette Jarrett. The silver-haired woman was reading a book to her son in the chief's office.

Lynette smiled warmly at her as Alicia stopped in the doorway. "Here's your mommy," she said to Charlie.

"Mommy!" He jumped down from the chair to wrap his arms around her legs. "I missed you."

Love tore through her heart and she scooped him up into her arms. "I missed you, too, bug." He laid his head on her shoulder. Over his head, Alicia smiled at Lynette. "Thank you. I hope it wasn't too much trouble for you to come to the station. I'm surprised the chief dragged you over here."

Lynette rose and touched Charlie's back. "Dwayne didn't drag me. I called to see how his day was going, and he said he was watching your little one. I had to come. I haven't seen my grandbabies in a while, and I was needing some little-boy time." She picked up a sack from the floor. "I brought books and treats. We were well entertained."

Grateful to the older woman, Alicia said, "I appreciate you keeping him busy."

"Of course. How's your father?"

"He's doing okay. Ornery and not wanting to do as the doctor tells him to keep his blood pressure under control. His diet is horrible. He's worse than a three-year-old when it comes to eating his veggies."

Lynette laughed. "Disguise them. It worked with my kids and grandkids."

"I will." Alicia glanced down and realized Charlie had fallen asleep in her arms. She needed to get him home.

Leo stepped into the office with Chief Jarrett.

"Agent Gallagher," Jarrett said, "this is my wife, Lynette.

Lynette, Agent Gallagher is from the FBI and is helping on a case."

Lynette's smile widened. "Well, that's special. I don't think I've heard of the FBI visiting our small slice of life here. I hope you'll find Settler's Valley to your liking."

Leo blinked, clearly not sure how to take the older woman's words. "I'm only here until this case is solved. The town is quaint, though." He turned to Alicia. "Are you ready?"

She tucked in her chin. "For?"

"The chief said you live on the outskirts of town. True and I will escort you to make sure you arrive safely."

"That's not necessary," she said. "It's a twenty-minute ride at best. We'll be fine." She could just imagine what her father would think if she brought home a federal agent.

Leo's jaw visibly tightened. "Yes, you will be fine. I'll see to it."

"No. You don't have to do that."

Chief Jarrett cleared his throat. "If you're willing to wait an hour or so, I can have officers escort you, if you'd rather."

Alicia whipped her gaze to the chief. She had no intention of staying here any longer than she absolutely needed to. "That's not necessary. The killer is most likely long gone." At least she prayed so.

"We can't take that risk. He might come after you since he knows you've seen his face," Leo stated in a firm voice.

"But I've already talked to the police, so what good would coming after me do?"

"He could eliminate you as a witness."

Leo's dire words sent fear cascading down her spine. She'd had that same thought earlier in the woods, but had dismissed it as paranoia. But realizing that the FBI agent and the police chief both thought she was still in danger had her heart pounding. Better to be safe than sorry, as the saying went. "All right. Agent Gallagher, you may follow us home."

And she'd send him on his way once they were safely back at the ranch.

Leo kept the SUV a couple of car lengths from the tailgate of Alicia Duncan's little all-wheel-drive sport vehicle as they headed away from the police station. The kid had fallen asleep in his mother's arms. Leo had to admit the little boy was very cute. And so was Alicia. He liked her spunk. She may not have wanted an escort home, but she was smart enough to realize that she was still in danger.

It was slow going through town due to congestion. Cars and people were out as evening was setting in. The turn-of-the-century architecture gave the place a quaint feel though he'd noticed a new hospital complex on the way in. Settler's Valley was nestled in the shadow of the Blackthorn Mountains, and the Blackthorn River flowed down the middle of town.

Several bridges connected the two sides, some for pedestrians, and others for vehicles. Alicia turned off the main drag, traveling away from the river and town. They cruised at fifty miles an hour on a flat stretch of asphalt that had fenced pastureland on either side of the two-lane road.

Having never been to Wyoming before, Leo took in the countryside. It was similar to nearby Montana, but there were distinct differences, too. Like the huge, brown bison walking along the side of the road. True barked at the creatures as they passed by five or six of them.

The terrain became more wooded the longer they drove. They passed several turnoffs marked by mailboxes. Gravel driveways led to far-off ranches that could barely be seen. What would it be like to reside so far from civilization?

Leo had lived and worked on a ranch in Kansas as a teen, but it hadn't been that far from town. He'd been able to ride his bike back and forth to school and later college. Those had been the hardest and the best years of his life. If not for the ranch foreman, Ben Smith, Leo's life would have followed a different path. A less productive one.

After a series of foster homes, he'd run away from the last one at age fourteen. He'd lived on the streets for two years before landing in Andale, Kansas, on the outskirts of Wichita. Population, nine hundred.

In a back alley behind a diner, Ben had found him scrounging through the garbage looking for something to eat. Ben had dragged him to the Crescent Ranch, where he put Leo to work mucking out stalls in exchange for food and board. Ben had been the one to insist Leo enroll in the local high school. And later to apply for college and scholarship money.

Leo's gaze snagged on a dark-colored muscle car with tinted windows waiting at the end of a driveway. Not exactly the type of vehicle one would expect to see coming from a ranch. Leo figured a teenager was probably at the wheel. No adult male would purposely put such a sweet ride through the torture of a gravel drive.

As Alicia's car approached the driveway, the muscle car's headlights came on and its engine revved, the rumble unmistakable despite the fact Leo's windows were rolled up. True reacted to the rumble with a series of frantic barks.

The nerves in Leo's gut constricted. He pressed the accelerator, forcing the SUV to gain on Alicia's smaller one. He was right on her tail.

"Brace yourself," Leo called to the dog. Thankfully, the compartment housing True was compact and padded for the dog's safety.

Alicia's car crossed directly in front of the driveway. The muscle car's tires spun and gravel flew as the vehicle charged forward, the driver's intention clear. He was about to ram into her. Leo stomped on the gas and swerved around Alicia, putting his SUV between her and the muscle car. Leo tensed, bracing for impact.

The driver of the other vehicle jammed on his brakes, barely missing Leo's SUV, as Leo and Alicia zipped past him.

Slowing to allow Alicia to pull in front of him again, Leo twisted the wheel, bringing the SUV into a 180-degree spin so that he now faced the assailant's car. He hit the dash lights that set off the unmistakable police strobe. The muscle car peeled out, sending a tail of gravel flying through the air, and sped toward town. Leo hit the steering wheel with the palm of his hand, torn between wanting to give chase and the need to protect Alicia and her son.

Decision made, he made another, slower U-turn and caught up to Alicia. He used the vehicle's Bluetooth to call Chief Jarrett and reported the incident. Unfortunately, it had been too dark to make out the car's license plate.

"I'll have patrol officers searching for the car and

driver. Keep Alicia and Charlie safe, Agent Gallagher," Jarrett instructed with worry in his tone.

"Count on it." Leo hung up and followed Alicia when she turned off onto a long gravel drive that led past rolling grass pastures populated with horses. A solid-looking log-and-brick house sat at the end of the drive, along with two other outbuildings and a large barn.

He drew the SUV to a halt beside Alicia's smaller vehicle. She sat there not moving. Concern arced through him. He quickly got out and released True. The dog took a second to assess the area before racing off to a patch of grass.

Leo opened the driver's side door of Alicia's car. Her fingers were wrapped around the steering wheel and her breathing was shallow. Her long, wavy dark hair created a veil that blocked her face from his view. He touched her shoulder. "Alicia, it's okay. You're home. I'm not going to let anything happen to you."

She leaned her head back against the headrest. "If you hadn't been with us…"

"But I was," he said gently. He held out his hand. "Let's get Charlie inside."

She peeled her fingers from the steering wheel and took Leo's hand. Her skin was soft but cold as she curled her fingers around his. "Can you get him?"

He swallowed back the terror the request sent spiraling through him. Two decades had passed since he'd last held a child in his arms. The last one had been his little sister the day she died. Guilt clawed up his throat. He took a shuddering breath and opened the back passenger door.

After releasing the buckle on Charlie's car seat, he cautiously lifted the sleeping boy into his arms, careful to keep the child's leg from catching on the holstered gun at his waist, and held him close to his chest with one arm. His heart hurt but he pushed through the pain to wrap his free arm around Alicia to help her toward the front door. True trotted over and stayed at his side.

The front door opened before they could climb the four stairs to the porch. True growled and positioned himself in front of Leo.

A grizzled man with gray hair, dressed in a plaid flannel shirt, jeans and cowboy boots, stood there with a shotgun in his gnarled hands. No doubt Harmon Howard, Alicia's father.

Leo stiffened. He'd been an agent long enough to recognize the protective gleam in the man's eyes, and he knew better than to make any sudden moves or the situation could get out of hand fast.

"Who are you?" The old man's jaw jutted forward. "What are you doing with my daughter and grandson?"

FOUR

"**D**ad! Put that thing away. You'll scare Charlie," Alicia admonished in a hushed tone to the man consuming the doorway of the ranch house, his shotgun leveled at Leo's chest.

The old man was doing a good job of setting Leo's nerves on edge, too. Tension knotted in his gut. Even though Alicia's father didn't have his finger on the trigger, Leo handed the sleepy child to his mother and then tucked them both behind him.

He'd rather take the hit square in the chest than allow anything to happen to anyone in his care. He wished he'd thought to wear a flak vest, but he hadn't anticipated facing down the barrel of a shotgun.

His elbow nudged his sidearm, but he kept his hand from reaching for the weapon. Best to take a less threatening stance. Keep things calm. He held up his hands, palms out. "Sir, please, lower your weapon."

True's menacing growl echoed in the stillness of the evening air.

"Leave it," Leo instructed. The last thing he needed was for True to tangle with Mr. Howard.

"Mister, you didn't answer my question," Harmon

Howard grumbled, but lowered the barrel toward the floor. His gaze bounced between True and Leo. "Who are you?"

"Agent Leo Gallagher of the FBI."

Harmon's lip curled. His dark blue gaze jumped to Alicia. "Another one? You don't learn from your mistakes, do you?" With that proclamation, Harmon did an about-face and disappeared inside the house.

Relief eased the stranglehold of tension in Leo's body and allowed his curiosity to pique. He glanced at Alicia. A blush tinged her cheeks. Her late husband had been a police officer in Tacoma, Washington. "Is your father against law enforcement in general?"

Alicia grimaced. "Not normally. Only my late husband."

Apparently her father wasn't a fan of Jeff Duncan's. Why?

Leo forced the question and the curiosity aside. No matter how attractive and compelling he found the pretty Alicia, he had no intention of letting anything get personal between them. The family dynamics here weren't any of his business.

His job was to protect the lady and her son and bring a criminal to justice before he killed anyone else. Then Leo could get back to searching for his friend Jake and for the low-life criminal Angus Dupree.

Alicia sighed. "I'm sorry. He's not the friendliest of men."

"He's protective. That's a good thing in this situation," Leo returned gruffly, glad that she had someone in her life that was willing to stand up on her behalf.

Everyone deserved a champion in their life. And

the fact that it was her father pleased him for her sake. He didn't have any good memories of his own father.

Leo put his hand to the small of her back and urged her up the steps. "Come on. Let's get you two inside."

True's nails clicked on the wooden porch planks. They crossed the threshold and entered the house. The savory aroma of beef coming from a pot simmering on the stove made Leo's mouth water. He hadn't eaten anything since before his run that morning. The toast with almond butter and coffee had sustained him until now.

True sniffed the air and licked his chops. "Lie down," Leo commanded. He'd retrieve True's food supply after he settled everyone in the house.

The canine lay down across the threshold of the door, but his gaze remained alert.

A warm blaze in the brick fireplace at the far end of the room chased away the evening chill. Plush leather chairs faced a wide-screen television. Harmon sat in one chair watching a baseball game, the sound turned way down. Leo was thankful the shotgun was nowhere to be seen. Hopefully the weapon was locked safely away. Leo would have a chat with the older man about it later.

The living room was decorated with Western paraphernalia. A large wagon wheel with small flickering votive candles on the horizontal beams dangled at the end of a thick rope from the tall ceiling. Several woven Native American blankets in bright colors hung on the large walls, giving the space a homey feel.

Stairs led to a loft area filled with toys and where Leo assumed the bedrooms were located. To the left was a nicely appointed kitchen with blond cabinetry and a dining table with four lattice-back chairs.

"I'll take Charlie upstairs for a short nap before dinner," Alicia said in a soft voice.

"I don't want a nap," Charlie groaned, sounding eerily similar to his grandfather, though his yawn belied his words.

So cute. Leo melted a little inside.

Before Alicia could move away, Charlie reached out his arms for Leo, snagging him around the neck and making a deft maneuver from his mother's embrace to Leo's arms. Charlie nestled his head against Leo's chest. Emotion constricted Leo's breath. The slight weight of the boy barely registered, but the warmth spreading through his chest made him ache. He attempted to pry Charlie away but the child hung on.

"Charlie, honey, let go of Agent Gallagher," Alicia said gently.

"Did you know that you grow when you sleep?" Leo asked the boy.

Charlie lifted his head and peered at Leo with doubt. "Really?"

"Yep. So every time you nap or sleep at night, you're getting bigger."

"I'm a big boy," Charlie said, his little face serious.

Leo smiled as a tenderness he hadn't experienced in a long time gripped him. "Yes, you are. But you want to keep getting bigger, right?"

With a solemn nod, Charlie extended his arms toward his mother.

Alicia took Charlie and set him on her hip. Her blue gaze held Leo's. "Thank you."

He winked. "You're welcome."

More pink heightened the contours of her high cheekbones. So pretty. He liked how natural she was as a mom and as a woman. She hurried upstairs with her son. Her long, lean legs moved with athletic grace, and her unbound, long dark hair bounced with each step. Leo watched them disappear from sight with a strange yearning that he didn't quite know what to do about, then turned his attention to the man in the chair. "Mr. Howard."

Alicia's father swiveled his recliner toward Leo and eyed him with overt suspicion. "You didn't answer my other question. What are you doing with my daughter and grandson?"

Leo braced his feet apart. These innocent people were in danger. He would do whatever it took to keep them safe. He couldn't let history repeat itself. "Alicia and Charlie are in danger."

Harmon jerked upright in his chair. "What have you gotten my family into?"

Holding up a hand, Leo said, "Alicia witnessed a crime."

The man blanched. "What crime?"

There was no reason to keep the truth hidden. "A homicide."

The older man sucked in a sharp breath. "Whose?"

"We don't have an identity on the victim yet. I'm sure we will soon."

Fear clouded Harmon's eyes. "But the killer knows Alicia and Charlie saw what happened?"

Anxiety thudded in Leo's gut. "Only Alicia witnessed the crime. The perp has already made two attempts on her life. He shot at her but she managed to get to the police station unharmed. And the other attempt was on the way out here. He tried to T-bone her car, but I blocked him with my SUV."

Harmon ran a vein-lined hand over his bristled jaw. He was visibly shaken. "This isn't good." His scowl darkened. "What are you doing to protect them?"

Everything he could. He prayed it would be sufficient. "I'm here and will stay until the perpetrator is caught. You have my word."

Harmon made a noise in his throat. "Why should we trust you? The last man who told me I could trust him with my daughter was a scoundrel of the worst kind." He rose and stared down at Leo.

Leo imagined in his younger days Harmon Howard was a man to contend with, though now his shoulders were slightly stooped. Age was taking its toll on the man. Leo held Harmon's gaze even as his mind grappled with that revealing statement about Alicia's deceased husband. Again curiosity bubbled but he tamped it down. None of his business.

True scrambled to his feet, sensing the mounting pressure in the room. Leo gestured with his hand for True to stay put.

Lips thinning, Harmon growled, "I can protect my family. You and your dog can leave."

"Not happening." He couldn't let anything happen to these people on his watch. "We can work together to keep your family safe or you can stay out of my way."

Harmon narrowed his gaze. "Like to be in control, do you?"

Leo had heard that comment before. He couldn't deny it. To be good at his job, he had to maintain control. The acrid burn of failure twisted in his stomach, reminding him he hadn't been able to control the situation that resulted in Jake's abduction.

Or in Leo's sister's death.

Harmon snorted. "You've got gumption, I'll give you that. Better than that louse she married."

Leo wasn't sure how to respond to the older man's pronouncement. Thanking him didn't seem right. Whatever the man's problem with Alicia's late husband had nothing to do with Leo or why he was here. He would not get involved in the personal lives of his charges. "Do you have a problem with me staying here until we apprehend the suspect?" Though he'd have to clear this with his boss. Leo was sure Max would want him to keep these people from harm.

Seeming to consider, Harmon finally shook his head. "No. We've got a spare room you can use."

Taking that as an invitation, some of the tension drained from Leo's shoulders. He'd rather work with Harmon than work against him. True must have sensed the shift in Leo's mood because he lay back down. "Good. You wouldn't happen to have a map showing the ranch's access points, would you?"

Harmon glanced toward the stairs then back at Leo with a gleam in his eyes. "Come with me." He led the way toward a room beneath the stairs.

The small space was a den of sorts that apparently also served as a bedroom. A twin bed was pushed up against the wall, beside it a chest of drawers with bits of plaid flannel sticking out.

Leo was glad to see a tall gun safe in the corner. The conversation about gun safety and children in the house wouldn't be necessary after all. There was a desk and a credenza loaded down with binders taking up the rest of the space. A braided rug softened their steps on the hardwood floor.

Harmon grabbed a roll of paper from a stack leaning against the safe. He unrolled it across the top of the desk and revealed a survey map of the ranch and the surrounding property. Leo studied it, noting the rendering was fairly recent, which was good. In the corner was the logo for a local realty company. "You planning to sell?"

Harmon's expression turned cagey. "Eventually."

Leo wondered how Alicia felt about that, then dismissed the musing. It wasn't any of his business. He turned his attention back to the drawing of the ranch.

The only road leading to the ranch house was the one they'd come in on. If the killer drove in, he'd be easy to spot. If he hiked in, True would sound an alarm.

"What's the total acreage?" Leo asked.

"Three hundred and two. We're smack-dab in the middle and it's all flat land."

Leo's cell phone rang. The caller ID showed it was his boss. "Excuse me. I have to take this."

He left the den and walked out of the house with True at his heels. The fading sun streaked the sky with fingers of gold and pink. The Howard ranch stretched in all directions. Horses grazed in a fenced paddock. Off in the distance, the Blackthorn Mountain range created a stunning silhouette against the evening sky.

He answered the call. "Gallagher."

"Christy said you found what you were looking for," Max West said.

"Yes, sir." Leo kept his gaze on the driveway that led to the main road. True sniffed around the small yard. "The witness led us to the body dump site. The diver pulled a woman out of the river. She's with the county coroner now. It wasn't Esme Dupree. But she could have been her doppelgänger."

"That corroborates what the US Marshals have told me. They confirmed Esme has been in hiding in the state of Wyoming."

His gut clenched. "That makes sense. A note was pinned to the victim's clothes. 'It's not sisterly to snitch, Esme.'"

Max growled. "A sick way of sending a message."

"Angus is trying to scare Esme out of testifying by killing a woman who looks like her," Leo said as he watched True disappear around the corner of the house.

"Someone called the marshals service, impersonating me, and tricked the marshals into revealing Esme was in Wyoming. The marshals are moving her from her current location."

He didn't envy them the task. "Is she safe?"

"As long as she stays in WITSEC she'll be safe."

"The killer knows about my witness and has already made two attempts at silencing her. I should stay here until the guy is caught."

Silence met his statement. "All right," Max finally said. "Keep me apprised and stay safe."

"Yes, sir." Leo hung up, grateful his boss had accepted Leo's need to stay and protect Alicia and her family. Getting into a contest of wills with Max wouldn't be a good idea for Leo, not if he hoped to advance in the Bureau.

"Who is Esme?"

Leo whipped around to find Alicia standing behind him. She'd left the door cracked open behind her. He hadn't heard her step out of the house. Not good. He needed to stay alert, keep his senses sharp.

He inhaled, catching a whiff of her scent, slightly floral and citrusy, that made him think of tropical islands, warm sandy beaches and crystal-blue oceans. His mouth dried. She'd changed from her fishing clothes into soft-looking lounge pants and a matching zipped-up jacket in a rich emerald that deepened the color of her ice-blue eyes.

Her dark hair was captured in the back by a shiny barrette, the long ends streaming over her shoulders. Her peaches-and-cream skin looked dewy as if she'd recently washed her face. One of her dark eyebrows rose as she waited for an answer. He'd been caught staring like a hormonal teenager.

He cleared his throat and turned his gaze to the horizon. "No one to concern yourself with."

She moved to stand next to him and folded her arms over her chest. "Don't patronize me. You thought the woman in the river would be this Esme person. But she wasn't. Who is Esme and why is someone trying to kill her?"

Exhaling roughly, Leo ran a hand through his hair. "I can't reveal the details of an ongoing investigation."

"I'm a part of this investigation now." Soft pink lips pressed together. "My late husband kept me in the dark about a lot of things. I won't let that happen again. I deserve to know what's going on since the killer now has me in his sights."

Interesting tidbit about her husband. But once again, he pushed his curiosity aside. He didn't want to know. Though she was right—she was now in the assassin's crosshairs.

Leo had to be careful not to compromise the case by revealing too much, but Alicia did deserve to know as much as he could tell her. He scanned the landscape, looking for any telltale signs of an intruder. "Esme Dupree is a key witness in an investigation and is set to testify against a criminal mastermind in a murder trial. He wants her stopped."

"You mean dead." Her voice shook slightly, drawing his gaze. A breeze lifted the ends of her hair as she looked off into the distance as if imagining the horrors yet to be faced. "If you catch this guy who dumped the woman in the river, I'll have to testify, won't I?"

He wouldn't sugarcoat what needed to be done. "Yes, you will. And when I capture this thug, he will lead me to the mastermind." And ultimately Jake.

Please, Lord, let him still be alive.

She pinned him with her gaze. "How do you know this guy is just a thug and not the ringleader?"

"Because the man wouldn't do his own dirty work."

"Will I be in danger from the criminal mastermind?" Her tone rose an octave.

"No. There'd be no reason for anyone else to come after you." He picked apart the growing shadows created by the fading evening light. "Once we bring the victim's murderer to justice, your part will be done."

She let out a breath. "If he doesn't succeed in silencing me first, you mean."

He put a hand on her shoulder, noticing the slender angles and planes of her physique. She was a tall woman, nearly matching his height. And fit. He liked that about her. But there was a vulnerability to her that made him want to protect her. "That's not going to happen, Alicia. I won't let it."

She shifted back slightly only to freeze, as if she was initially going to move away from his touch but something stopped her. "I know how this works, Agent Gallagher," she said. "You can't guarantee our safety."

Dropping his hand to his side, he assured her, "I can do everything in my power to keep you safe."

"But you're leaving. You have a job to do out there." She swept her hand toward the horizon.

"I'm staying put until we catch this guy."

She frowned, confusion clouding her gaze. "You mean you're staying in town, right?"

Leo had the feeling she wasn't going to be amenable to him bunking in the house. He widened his stance, prepared to convince her. "No. I'll be staying here. Your father has already offered the spare room."

Her pretty eyes widened. She drew herself up and regarded him with a mix of curiosity and speculation. "Did he, now? He's not usually so accommodating."

"I heard that," Harmon bellowed from inside the house. "Dinner's ready."

Alicia's lips twisted in a rueful smile. "Hungry?"

"Starved." And grateful she hadn't argued with him. She was smart enough to know he was her best defense against the thug wanting her dead. At least he hoped he was.

"Good." She stepped back inside. Leo whistled and True came bounding around the side of the house. They entered and Leo motioned for True to settle by the door.

"Do you have a bowl for water?" Leo asked Alicia.

"Of course." She went to the kitchen and opened a cupboard to pull out a metal mixing bowl. She filled it with water from the tap and set it down in front of the dog. True eagerly lapped at the water. "I don't have dog food but I do have some leftover roasted chicken. Would he eat that?"

Grateful for her thoughtfulness, Leo smiled. "I have supplies in my truck but he'd happily have a snack."

Alicia opened the refrigerator and took out a plastic container of cooked chicken breasts. Handing it to him, she said, "Take out however much you think would be good for him."

He took out one large breast. Alicia pulled out a cutting board and handed him a knife. He chopped the breast up into bite-size pieces.

"Here." She offered him a paper plate to put the food on.

"Thank you." He set down the food next to the water. True stared at him, waiting for permission. "Eat." The dog sniffed the chicken before gently taking a piece in his mouth and chewing.

Alicia laughed. "He's so polite."

"He's well trained," he countered. "We have two excellent dog trainers at our headquarters in Billings."

"Is that where you're from?" she asked.

"Not originally."

"Where, then?" She handed him plates to take to the table.

"Kansas." Uncomfortable talking about himself, he set the plates on the table and took a seat across from Harmon. "What about Charlie?"

"He'll eat when he wakes up," Alicia replied as she went to the stove. She carried over the pot of stew and set it on a pot holder in the middle of the table. "Help yourself."

He couldn't help but watch her as she retrieved a loaf of garlic bread from the oven and cut the loaf into slices. She moved with efficient grace. A stray tendril of midnight-black hair escaped her barrette and fell over her cheek. She pushed it back with her forearm.

Aware of Harmon's sharp gaze, Leo turned his attention to the black cast-iron pot and used the steel ladle to dish out a bowl of stew. The appetizing scent wafting from the bowl made his stomach growl.

Harmon filled his bowl and then filled Alicia's. She brought over a basket filled with the bread slices and offered it to Leo. He took a couple of pieces.

The food was good and filling. The stew was savory with spices that Leo couldn't name but enjoyed. The meat was tender and the vegetables firm. "This is the best meal I've had in a long time, Harmon. Thank you. You're a great cook."

The older man snorted. "I don't cook. Alicia made it before she left to take Charlie fishing this morning."

"Then thank you, Alicia." He grinned at her, impressed. "I appreciate your culinary talent."

A blush heightened on the contours of her cheeks. "I'm glad to hear you enjoyed it. That makes me happy."

He was glad he could make her happy. The way she looked at him, as if trying to decide if he was telling the truth, had him wondering just what kind of man her late husband had been. Apparently not a stellar one if he was to believe her father.

"I aim to please," he replied huskily as he held her gaze.

She blinked and tucked in her chin. "You don't have a family of your own waiting for you at home?"

Not even close. Romantic entanglements weren't part of his life plan. Too much responsibility. The risk of failure too high. "No." Time to steer her in a different direction. "I understand you're a teacher. That must take a lot of patience."

Her mouth lifted at the corners. It was clear that his change in subject wasn't lost on her. "I am. Or was. I'm taking some time off."

"That's understandable." She'd lost her husband six

months ago. Leo would imagine she was still in the grieving process. Charlie, too. Leo ached for them both.

True leaped to his feet with a growl.

Pulse jumping, Leo rose. The dog faced the door with his ears forward and tail raised, and bristled with tension. All signs that True detected a threat. Hand on his gun, Leo said to Alicia and Harmon, "Hide in the den."

Going to the front door, Leo positioned himself to one side and cracked open the door to peer outside. He didn't see a threat. But that didn't mean there wasn't one.

A whirring noise drew closer and louder with each second.

"What is that?" Alicia asked. She'd moved to stand behind her dad's chair. Neither had done as he'd instructed. Frustration pounded at his temples.

Harmon's brow furrowed. "Sounds like a swarm of bees."

Leo clenched his jaw. "A drone." Which meant the killer was on the property and attempting to get the lay of the land.

To True, Leo commanded, "Guard." To Alicia, he said, "Get out of sight."

A surge of adrenaline pumped through his veins as he hurried from the house to his vehicle. Leo popped open the back, where he kept his gear, and grabbed a set of NVGs—night-vision goggles. He searched the now-darkened sky.

The drone was high and coming from the southwest. No doubt the drone had a camera. Leo wouldn't put it past the Dupree syndicate to have access to military-grade equipment. Anxiety twisted in his gut. Could the drone now flying over the Howard ranch be weaponized?

FIVE

Adrenaline surged through Leo, making his heart pound. He couldn't take any chances that the small black four-rotor drone hovering over the Howard ranch house had been fitted with the ability to fire rockets or machine-gun rounds.

He needed to bring down the drone while it was high enough not to cause any damage to the house before anything bad happened to the Howard family.

From the back of his SUV, he grabbed his FBI-issued assault rifle. He set it to one-round bursts. Through the night-vision goggles, Leo sighted the rifle on the buzzing drone and moved his finger to the trigger.

The drone suddenly jerked sideways and dipped below the roofline before Leo could take the shot. Frustration ripped through his veins. Clearly whoever was piloting the drone had spotted him.

Inside the house, True's frantic barking raised the hair on Leo's arms. The drone had the dog spooked. With adrenaline flooding his system, Leo raced to the house and circled around to the back. The drone hung in the air, level with the kitchen window and the camera pointed inside the house. This close, Leo was thankful not to see any sort of weapon attached to the drone.

Shooting down the remote-controlled device this close to the house would be too risky in case there were hidden defensive explosives inside the casing. Leo put the rifle's strap over his shoulder and lunged at the drone with both hands, hoping to manually incapacitate the thing. The flying object zipped sideways out of his reach before soaring away.

He tracked it with the NVGs until it disappeared. Anger simmered low in his gut. After removing the goggles, he reached for his phone and dialed the authorities.

"Settler's Valley police department. What's your emergency?" the dispatcher asked, her voice clipped and professional.

After identifying himself, Leo said, "I need to speak to Chief Jarrett."

"I'll put you through," she said and the line went silent.

A minute passed before Jarrett answered. "Agent Gallagher, has something happened?" Concern darkened the man's voice.

"We're all fine." Inside the house True peered back at him through the window. "A drone flew over the Howards' home. It was a quad-copter with a camera on board and came from southwest of the ranch. These things have a range of thirty miles but if it was livestreaming, which I'm guessing it was because it used tactical maneuvers, the controller could be a lot closer."

"I've got two deputies out that way now. I'll have them scour the perimeter around the ranch."

"Thank you, though I doubt they'll find anything.

The suspect knows I'm onto him. He's not going to wait around to be apprehended."

"Doesn't hurt to have them make a sweep. And I can have officers go back out in daylight to see if they can find anything to lead us to the suspect."

He scanned the inky shadows of the barn, the horse corral and beyond to the landscape. That would have to do. For now. He glanced back to the window looking for signs of Alicia and her father. "Any sightings on the muscle car?" Obviously, hiding out on the ranch wasn't a permanent solution. They needed to find this guy before he hurt anyone else. Especially the lovely Alicia and her child and father. Leo wouldn't let anything happen to the Howard family.

"None yet. If he headed into town, you'd think someone would have remembered a car like that."

"Right." Most of the vehicles Leo had seen driving around town were older pickups and tricked-out trucks and SUV types. Winters in this part of Wyoming could be brutal. "Let me know if your officers find anything."

Leo hung up and trotted back to his vehicle. He replaced his tactical gear, then grabbed his overnight to-go bag, along with True's supply bag and an extra clip of ammo for his holstered weapon. Glancing up at the night sky, he searched for signs of the drone. Seeing nothing, he closed his eyes to listen for the telltale hum of the unmanned aircraft, but heard only the nasally *peent* call of a nighthawk flying over the ranch.

The absence of horns or human life was eerie after having lived the past decade in the bustling metropolis of Billings. Leo had forgotten how peaceful the country could be and would have savored the tranquillity if it wasn't for some madman out there determined to assassinate pretty Alicia Duncan.

Deciding he needed to be ready and have his rifle with him in case the drone returned, he hefted the weapon's case from the back of the SUV and took it with him to the house, secure in the knowledge the biometric lock programmed to his fingerprint wouldn't allow any curious minds to open the case.

He entered through the front door and set True's bag and the rifle case on the floor, out of the way until he could take them to the guest room. All was quiet. True greeted him with a nudge of his nose. Leo scrubbed the dog behind the ears as he looked around for his hosts.

But Alicia and Harmon were not in the living room, dining room or kitchen. Concern arced through him. Had the drone been a distraction to take him away from the family? No. True would never have allowed it. But the utter silence of the house after the chaos of the drone nearly wrecked him. Acid burned in his gut. "Alicia!"

Harmon's den door opened. Alicia ran out carrying Charlie. Relief nearly buckled Leo's knees. They had hidden as he'd asked. He braced his feet apart to keep from staggering forward to fold the pair in his arms. He didn't want to contemplate why he had the urge to begin with. Harmon followed his daughter out of the room, carrying his shotgun.

The fear on Alicia's face knotted Leo's chest.

"Is it gone?" Her voice shook slightly.

"Yes. Chief Jarrett is sending officers in the direction it came from." He adjusted his to-go bag on his shoulder. "The drone had a camera attached to its base. It was doing recon on the ranch."

Alicia hugged Charlie closer. "Are we safe?"

"Yes." He hated that she questioned his determination to protect them. "True will alert if there's another threat," Leo assured her. He needed her to trust him to do his job.

"Thank you." In the pale depths of her blue eyes, he saw gratitude, sadness and a hint of desperation that tore at him.

"I'm hungry, Mommy," Charlie said, drawing their attention.

"Okay, sweetie." Alicia took Charlie to the dining table and set him on a chair. "I'll warm you some mac and cheese."

Leo turned to Harmon. "That spare room?"

"It's upstairs," he said. "Let me lock this up first." The old man shuffled back into the den, returning a moment later. He paused at the bottom of the stairs and looked up, as if preparing himself.

"Dad, I'll show Agent Gallagher to his room," Alicia said as she secured Charlie in a seat at the table. "You can warm up some mac and cheese."

Visibly relieved, Harmon walked slowly to the kitchen.

Leo raised an eyebrow at Alicia.

"Bad knees," she whispered.

"Ah." Leo nodded to Harmon and picked up his and True's bags and the weapon case.

Alicia's gaze dropped to the long hard-side case carrying his assault rifle, and then her eyes met his.

"It has a secure lock on it," he assured her before she could protest. Though she seemed okay with her father's shotgun, what Leo carried was far more deadly.

She pressed her lips together and nodded, then gave Charlie a quick hug as if assuring herself he'd be okay while she left the room.

Leo headed to the stairs with True at his heels. "You stay here, buddy," Leo said to his canine. "Help guard Charlie."

Alicia brushed past him, her scent swirling in the air and perking up his senses. He hesitated a moment to allow her to proceed to the second floor, careful to keep his gaze from tracing her alluring curves. No matter how pretty he thought Alicia was, he wasn't here to indulge in an attraction. She was his to protect, nothing more.

"Agent Gallagher."

Alicia's soft voice stopped him on the upstairs landing. "Please, call me Leo. We're going to be in close quarters for a while."

She nodded but her eyebrows pinched together. "Leo. I appreciate what you're doing for us."

"Keeping you and your family safe is my job, Alicia."

"And finding the man who wants your witness dead," she pointed out.

"Yes, that, too."

"I'll pray that you find him." Her words wrapped around him. The common bond of faith pleased him. He could use all the help he could get. And the more people praying the better.

"I will, too."

The corners of her generous mouth curved upward. "Good to know."

The power of her smile rocked him back on his heels. His chest tightened. She was appealing in a wholesome way that he found compelling. Temptation to open his heart flared white-hot, but he quickly tamped it down. Not going there.

He couldn't let himself develop any sort of feelings for this woman. It wouldn't be fair to her. Yet he could barely contain the yearning from arcing through him to discover if her lips were as soft as they looked, to learn if she was as nice as she seemed. He had to force his feet to move to follow her down the hall instead of turning tail and running away.

He didn't do commitment. He didn't do relationships. There was too much at stake to allow any sort of romance in his life. The sad fact was, he didn't know how.

She pushed open the door to reveal a spacious guest room with a queen-size bed decorated with a multicolored quilt and several pillows. A dresser stood next to the window and an armchair was perched in the corner. A small cherrywood desk and chair stood beneath the curtained window.

Growing up, he'd never had a home like this. There'd been no guest room in his house. No guests, either. His dad had been abusive and his mom too busy ducking his fists to entertain. She barely had the wherewithal to care for her two children.

Alicia gestured to two closed doors. "There's a walk-in closet and a bathroom. You'll find towels under the sink."

"This is nice. Thank you for your hospitality." Leo set his bag on the bed. "Where do you sleep?"

Color raced up Alicia's cheeks. "Charlie and I are at the other end of the hall."

Close enough to protect them should the need arise. But as he stared into her pale blue eyes, he wondered if he would be the one needing protection from his burgeoning feelings for this woman by the time all was said and done.

"I'll let you freshen up." Mortified at the realization that she was blushing, Alicia slipped from the room before Leo could respond to the sleeping arrangements.

Instead of going downstairs, she hurried down the hall to her room, where she closed the door and leaned against the cool wood. She put her hands to her hot cheeks.

Why was she blushing? It wasn't that she didn't trust Agent Leo Gallagher, but the man was too handsome for words. And charming. *So charming.* She didn't want to admit it but she found him extremely attractive. And kind and protective. Also good with Charlie. All wonderful traits.

But he scared her in ways she didn't like.

She would not let herself form any attachment to the agent. She'd have to make sure to protect Charlie as well. The last thing either of them needed was another man to let them down. She'd had enough disappointment to last a lifetime. She wouldn't subject herself or her son to more.

With that resolve firmly in place, she left her room and went downstairs. Charlie sat in his booster seat at the dining table, eating his mac and cheese while her father did the dishes. True sat next to Charlie's chair.

The big dog turned his brown eyes toward her, his ears twitching and his tail thumping on the ground. Was he happy? She wasn't sure how she felt about having a dog in the house and so close to Charlie. The only animals she'd had growing up were horses and cows.

She moved to the table, stepping around the dog, and ruffled Charlie's hair. "Good job on your food."

"I was hungry," he said around a mouthful.

"No talking with food in your mouth," she chided gently.

Something wet nudged her hand. True had scooted

closer and pushed his nose into her. Tentatively, she patted the dog on the head. "Nice dog."

"He hasn't left Charlie's side," her dad observed as he draped a dish towel over his shoulder. He stood by the kitchen sink. The counters were spotless and the dishwasher loaded. She was thankful Dad didn't mind cleaning. "It's nice having a canine in the house. A good alarm system."

There was a wistfulness in his tone that made her curious. "Why didn't we ever have a dog?"

Sadness entered his gaze. "When your mom was a young girl she was attacked by a stray dog," Dad said. "Ever since then she'd been afraid of dogs. It didn't seem worth having one if it upset her."

Love for her father filled her heart. Alicia had hoped her marriage would be like her parents'. The fact that her marriage hadn't been, not by a long shot, left a raw, aching gash deep in her core. "I miss her."

Dad swallowed hard. "Me, too, sweetheart."

Leo came down the stairs, distracting her from her melancholy thoughts. He'd changed into comfortable-looking jeans that hugged his lean frame and a pull-over sweatshirt with the team logo for the Kansas City Chiefs emblazoned on the front. "True and I are going to do a perimeter check."

She liked how thorough he was. "Do you need a flashlight?"

"I've got one in the truck," he replied. "Are there wild animals around here I should be concerned about?"

"We get the occasional elk or mule deer," Dad informed him. "There have been sightings of mountain lions within Settler's Valley, but we haven't had one close to the house."

"Good to know," Leo muttered as his hand went to his hip as if searching for his sidearm. She wondered if it was concealed beneath the hem of his sweatshirt.

"I'll go out with you," Alicia said. "I need to check on the horses." She looked at her father. "Can you give Charlie his bath?"

"Of course," Dad replied evenly, though his gaze narrowed slightly.

Uncomfortable beneath the weight of his stare, her pulse jumped. There was no reason to feel self-conscious about the request. It wasn't like she was hoping to get Leo alone in the barn for a romantic tryst. She had to feed the horses and she'd prefer to have the agent close by. That was all.

She grabbed a down vest to ward off the evening chill and headed out the front door. Leo whistled and True left Charlie's side to follow Leo. The cool night air was refreshing on her face as she paused at the foot of the porch stairs. Leo strode to his SUV and returned a few minutes later with a high-powered flashlight. He'd clipped a leash on True's collar.

"How many horses do you own?" Leo asked as they made their way to the large barn, thirty feet from the house.

She undid the latch and slid the front barn door open. "We have three now." She flipped on the overhead lights.

The horses had already wandered in through their stall doors, which allowed them access to the paddock, and were waiting for their dinner. "We used to have ten, but when my mom fell ill, Dad sold them off along with the cattle to pay her doctor bills."

"I'm sorry for your loss," he murmured softly. "How long ago did she pass?"

Grief squeezed her heart. "It's been a little over four years now. Right as I learned I was pregnant with Charlie, Mom was diagnosed with lymphoma. It took her quickly." Drawn by the soft neighing of the horse, she went to the first stall.

"Guard," Leo told True. He looped his leash around the door latch before walking into the barn. He stopped beside Alicia.

"This is Stardust. She's mine." She petted the pretty dappled gray head sticking out over the half door.

Leo reached up to stroke the horse's neck. "How long have you had her?"

Moving to drag a fresh hay bale from the corner of the barn, she said, "She was my twelfth birthday present. I got her as a foal."

Reaching past her, Leo easily lifted the bale and took it to Stardust's stall. She opened the gate for him to set the hay inside. "I'm surprised you left her behind."

Guilt made her defenses rise. After closing the back paddock door to keep the horse in for the night, she shut the gate with too much force when she returned to Leo's side. "I didn't have a place to keep her in Tacoma."

She moved to the next stall, where a quarter horse named Apple waited for attention.

Leo dusted off his hands on his jeans. "What took you to Washington?"

"My late husband," she admitted. "Jeff had an aunt who lived in Tacoma. After high school we moved there. I enrolled in the University of Puget Sound while he went to the police academy in Burien."

"You married young." He walked away to grab another bale of hay and brought it over. She opened the gate and nudged Apple aside so he could set down the hay.

"Yes, we did. Too young, I now realize." She peered at him closely. "Have you been married?"

"No." He turned away to fetch another hay bale but not before she caught a flash of something. Pain? Regret? She wasn't sure.

"Ever come close?" she persisted as she secured the gate much more gently and moved to the last stall, where another quarter horse waited. Leo's movements became brisk, jerky. She could see the tension in his shoulders. She wasn't sure he was going to answer her, but she waited him out, stroking Brutus's neck. The stud horse buried his nose in her hair.

When Leo moved closer to deposit the hay bale in the stall, she saw the tightness in his jaw and the shuttered expression in his green eyes. "No," he finally said, his voice clipped.

She studied him in the dim light of the barn. He didn't seem inclined to expand on his answers. Her curiosity spiked but she really had no reason to want to know more about him. Except, she was putting her life and that of her son and father into his hands. It seemed prudent to learn a little bit about the man protecting them. "You're a Chiefs fan."

His eyes widened. "Yes. How did…?" He looked down at his shirt then grinned at her, making her breath stall in her lungs. "Oh, right," he said. "I'd forgotten I had this on. Can't be from Kansas and not root for the Chiefs."

"Where in Kansas?"

"I was born in Topeka but I spent my teen years on a horse ranch in Andale."

They had something in common. "You ride?"

"Of course."

The thought of the two of them off galloping across the ranch made her smile. She would like to see him on one of the horses. To see how he handled the large beast. But he wasn't here on holiday; he was here to keep her alive. Her smile faded and a shiver tripped across her neck. She locked up behind them and searched the shadows for danger. To distract herself from the peril lurking beyond the confines of the ranch proper, she asked, "Are your parents still in Andale?"

"They were never in Andale," he said, his voice taking on a hard edge. "I haven't seen my parents since I was eight."

Shock took her breath away. She worked through his words. So young to lose his family. "I'm sorry. Did they pass on?"

His expression stony, he undid True's leash. "I have no idea. I was taken away from them and put into foster care."

Her heart hurt for him. What had his parents done to warrant losing their child? Had he been abused? Neglected? She wanted to reach out a hand to comfort him, but the firmness of his jaw and the tautness in his shoulders led her to believe he wouldn't welcome the gesture. "That's horrible."

"It was for the best," he said softly. There was a note of torment in his voice that ratcheted up her desire to soothe him.

He took her by the elbow and steered her toward the house. "True and I will escort you back."

They walked in silence. Alicia struggled to come up with something to say. Questions about Leo's life peppered her mind but she held back. He obviously didn't want to discuss his childhood. She had the feeling something bad had happened. Something that still haunted him.

Just as they reached the porch stairs, his cell phone rang. He paused. She hesitated, hoping it was Chief Jarrett calling to say they'd found the killer.

"Gallagher," he answered. Though the porch light barely extended to where they stood, she could see the agitation in Leo's face as he listened to the person on the other side of the line. Apprehension fluttered through her.

After a moment, he said, "Here? In Wyoming?"

He glanced at her then set his jaw in a firm line. "I have to do a perimeter check of the ranch house. Then I'll get to my computer." He punched the off button with a fierce jab.

"What's wrong?" Before he could respond she continued, "And don't tell me 'nothing.' I can see that something has upset you."

He remained silent. An inner struggle played across his face. His jaw firmed.

Frustration itched up her neck. "Listen, I know you think you're protecting me by staying silent, but not knowing what's going on will make me crazy. My late husband kept the ugly side of his work from me. I knew it was there, I knew his work was dangerous, but I was still blindsided when I learned he'd been undercover at the time of his death. He didn't trust me to handle the truth." He hadn't loved her enough to stay faithful, either. She pushed aside the old hurt to focus on the man in front of her.

A heartbeat later, Leo blew out a breath. "A week ago one of my coworkers, my friend Jake, was kidnapped by the same men who are after Esme Dupree."

She braced herself. Had he learned of his friend's demise? "Is he...?"

"An anonymous tip came into the headquarters in Billings. Jake has been spotted here in Wyoming."

"At least you know he's alive," she said. Shouldn't he be glad for that?

"Yes. I am thankful to know he lives. But I fear Angus Dupree is making Jake help them find Esme."

A shiver of dread raced down her spine. "By 'making' you mean torturing him?"

"Unfortunately, I do."

And this same man pulled the strings on the killer she'd seen at the river. The man hunting her.

SIX

Leo hurried Alicia inside the house, anxious to get the perimeter check done so he could fire up his computer to video chat with the FBI Tactical K-9 Unit in Billings.

Once Alicia was safely out of sight, he and True walked a brisk path around the house, barn and outbuildings. He didn't like how open and exposed they were here in the middle of the flat plains with the mountains in the far distance. He mentally noted possible hiding places close to the house, where a threat could lurk.

An old tractor. Stacks of hay bales beneath a tarp. A classic '50s Chevy truck that appeared to be in prime condition. The barn. The equipment shed. All places that could prove problematic. If he had access to resources, he'd set up a surveillance camera and sensors. But all he had was himself and his partner. It had to be enough.

He'd address these potential hazards in the light of day. Maybe set up some sort of rudimentary alarm system with cans or bells.

His thoughts turned to Jake and his insides twisted into a knot. The news his boss had delivered echoed inside his head like thunder rolling across the clear night sky.

Jake was alive.

That should have assuaged Leo's guilt just as Alicia suggested, but the thought of the unspeakable horrors being done to Jake to get him to betray the oath they'd taken the first day of training in Quantico made bile rise in Leo's throat. Alicia. Her words about her husband's lack of faith in her ability to handle the unsavory parts of his world had obviously hurt her. The fierce way she'd insisted she was to be kept in the loop had increased Leo's respect for her.

Too often civilians wanted to cling to their ignorance when it came to the more repellent and nasty side of law enforcement. Dealing with drug lords, human traffickers and criminals without a conscience wasn't for the faint of heart.

Leo took his vow to support and defend the United States from enemies, foreign and domestic, seriously. The Dupree syndicate was a blight on the American people. Angus Dupree and his nephew, Reginald, had to be stopped. With Esme's help, Reginald would be in prison for a long time. It was up to the team to capture Angus Dupree and end his reign of terror.

And Jake needed to be rescued.

From the front porch of the Howard ranch, Leo whistled for True, who'd made a beeline for a patch of grass a minute ago. The dog came running from the direction of the paddock. No doubt the smell of the horses had his nose twitching.

With True at his side, Leo entered the house. A small dynamo ran straight at him, catching him around the knees, rocking him back several steps. True, obviously sensing no threat, lay down in front of the door.

Barely able to hold on to his balance as surprise washed

over him, Leo stared down at Charlie's head resting on his thigh. The boy was dressed in navy-colored footie pajamas with rockets soaring across the material. Emotions long buried, which he'd thought were forever forgotten, surged through him. Tenderness flooded his system. He placed a hand on Charlie's head. His dark hair was damp from his recent bath.

Leo's gaze met Alicia's.

Her luminous blue eyes were wide and worried. "Sorry. I don't know what's gotten into him."

"It's okay," Leo murmured to reassure her. He wondered where her anxiety stemmed from. Did she think he'd be upset by Charlie's exuberant welcome? Far from it. He couldn't explain the surge of fondness washing over him. Strange how quickly the child was getting under his skin. Gently, he smoothed a hand over the boy's head. "Hey, kiddo. Are you okay?"

The boy tilted his head back. His pale blue gaze, eyes so like his mother's, blinked up at him with earnest trust. Leo's heart ached. It had been so long since anyone had looked at him that way.

"Will you play I Spy with me?" Charlie asked.

"Honey, Agent… Leo isn't here to play. He's working." Alicia hurried forward to pry Charlie from around Leo's legs. To Leo, she whispered under her breath, "It's his new favorite game. A matching game."

"Ah." Leo squatted down in front of Charlie. Alicia's hands rested on the child's thin shoulders. Staring directly into the boy's face, Leo had to fight the constriction in his throat to get his words out. "I would love to play I Spy with you in the morning. Right now, I do have to work."

Charlie sighed. Obviously, he'd heard that phrase before. "Okay. In the morning."

The disappointment in the child's eyes speared through Leo. He didn't like letting the boy down. Or anyone, for that matter.

"Why don't you ask Grandpa to play with you?" Alicia steered the boy toward Harmon, who sat in his recliner watching another baseball game.

Leo rose and watched Charlie climb into Harmon's lap and lay his head against the older man's shoulder. A searing pain lodged itself in Leo's chest. Longing for what he knew he'd never allow himself to have flooded him. He'd determined long ago that fatherhood wasn't something he could ever risk. His baby sister was gone because he hadn't been able to care for her properly. He never wanted to be responsible for another child's life.

He jerked his gaze away to find Alicia watching him. He purposely cleared his expression, hoping she hadn't glimpsed his own private anguish.

"True will sound an alarm if anyone approaches the house," Leo told her. "I need to have a video call with my boss."

Alicia tugged on her bottom lip. There was a question in her eyes. Leo figured she wanted in on the call. But he couldn't offer without first clearing her presence with his boss, Max West.

After a moment, she appeared resigned to not being included and stepped aside so he could move to the stairs. At the top of the landing he glanced back to see she'd followed him to the foot of the staircase, her arms wrapped around her middle as if that was the only thing holding her together.

His heart squeezed tight. She was scared and feeling

vulnerable. He didn't blame her. This situation had to be frightening. He would do everything in his power to keep her, and her young child, safe.

As if she'd somehow sensed his thoughts, she straightened her spine and dropped her hands to her sides. Her chin lifted. She may be frightened but she had a core of steel. Good for her. He admired strength that came from character rather than might or power. He inclined his head in respect before going down the hall to the guest room.

Once there he set up his computer on the desk beneath the window. Within seconds of firing up the device, he was added to a video chat with the team back at headquarters. They were all seated around the conference table.

Ian sat between Julianne and Harper. The junior team members, Tim and Nina, sat across the table. Christina sat on Max's right, a notepad in front of her. Dylan sat on Max's left, his laptop open.

To them, he was a big head on the screen attached to the wall at the end of the room.

"Tell me what you know about Jake," Leo said to no one in particular.

"Like I told you earlier," Max said, "an anonymous call came in from a burner phone. The caller used some sort of voice-altering microphone, so we don't know if the person was male or female. The caller said we should look for Jake in Wyoming."

Though he'd already heard this, the news still burned like battery acid through his gut. "Did the caller give any hint where in the state to look for him? Wyoming's vast with lots of uninhabited land."

"No. No specifics," Dylan answered. "Here, let me play you the recording."

Dylan typed on the keypad of the laptop sitting in front of him. A second later a disembodied voice filled the air and came at Leo through his computer speakers.

"If you want to find your missing agent, head to Wyoming."

The line went dead.

"Have you isolated any background noise?" Leo asked, though he trusted Dylan would do everything possible to identify the caller.

"There is none," Dylan answered. "Whoever sent this recording knew how to make it untraceable."

"It has to be someone within the Dupree gang," Ian said.

Dissension in the ranks. That was gratifying and brought him a small measure of comfort. Maybe Jake had convinced one of his guards to help him. Leo had seen Jake use his charisma to get suspects to confess. The man was a smooth operator, especially with the ladies. Why not charm one of his jailers into making the call? Turning a discontented thug wouldn't be a stretch. That would be just like Jake.

"Considering the recent murder of a woman who looks like Esme, we should assume Dupree is somewhere close to where you are and therefore so is Jake," Max stated. "Julianne and I are headed your way. We'll spearhead the search for Jake and Angus Dupree from Settler's Valley."

Leo took the news in stride. The beauty of the team was they could operate from anywhere and could take cases across state lines while having the full resources of the Federal Bureau of Investigation at their fingertips.

Or rather, Dylan's, since he was their resident computer guru who could ferret out any bit of information within the cyber world they could ever need.

"Let me know when you hit town," Leo said. "We could meet you at the police station. I have a forensic artist coming in to work with Alicia on a sketch of the suspect at the river. She gave me a general description. Dark eyes, shaved head, not tall and bulky." Dylan typed into his computer as Leo talked.

"Alicia?" Ian raised an eyebrow. "Is she the witness?"

The image of the dark-haired beauty with her captivating blue eyes rose in his mind. There was a vulnerability about her that spoke to him nearly as much as her strength of character. She was a good mother, from what he could tell. She took care of her cantankerous father with patience and the horses, too. She held this place together. But who held *her* together?

"Yes. Alicia Duncan. Widow with a three-year-old son. She and the boy live with her elderly father on a medium-sized ranch in the middle of nowhere outside of Settler's Valley."

"You're there now?" Harper asked.

"I am. The guest room."

Julianne pushed her long dark braid over her shoulder and sat forward. "What have you told Alicia regarding the murder of the Esme look-alike?"

Leo lifted his chin. "Everything we know."

"Is that wise?" Ian questioned.

He met Max's gaze through the computer screen. "Alicia was with me when you called. I told her about Jake's abduction and the Duprees. She deserves to know why her and her family's lives are in danger."

Max nodded. "Any sign of the perp?"

"Not in the flesh but he's out there." Leo gave them the lowdown on the drone and his suspicion that the suspect was casing the ranch, looking for a weakness. A way to gain access to Alicia. *He won't find one*, Leo silently pledged and sent up a quick prayer that the good Lord above would make sure he could keep that promise.

"Is there any way to track the drone?" Max asked Dylan. "I assume the pilot of the unmanned aerial craft is using a wireless remote to operate it."

"Unfortunately, there's not at this time, but soon something will be invented and released that will allow for remote tracking," Dylan told him.

"Which is no help in this situation," Max grumbled.

There was a knock on the bedroom door.

"Excuse me, guys," Leo said to the group on his laptop screen. He rose and opened the door. Alicia, holding Charlie on her hip, stood there. Instead of being irritated by the interruption, he was strangely pleased to see them even as concern rose. "Is everything okay?"

Alicia's gaze darted past Leo to the laptop and back again. "Yes…sorry. Charlie insists on saying good-night to you."

The boy launched himself into Leo's arms. He smelled of the fresh clean children's shampoo and bubble-gum toothpaste. Holding the boy close made Leo's chest ache. Protectiveness blasted through him. He tightened his hold on the boy.

The feel of Charlie's tiny arms around his neck, the rapid beat of the child's heart against his own and the scents of childhood were now imprinted on Leo's mind. He'd remember this feeling for a long time to come.

"You have good sleep," he said to the child, his voice thick. "In the morning we'll play I Spy."

Charlie nodded and yawned. "Okay. G'night, Agent Leo."

Heart melting, Leo gave the boy a squeeze then handed him back to his mother. Though he had to admit, he missed the unconditional love of a child. "Good night, kiddo."

Over Charlie's head, Alicia's soft gaze took Leo's breath away. The trust and gratitude in her eyes scored him clean through. His gut twisted with alarm. He had to be careful not to allow himself to become attached to these two, or let Alicia believe there could be anything more than just a temporary job keeping them together.

"Good night, Leo," she murmured before slipping away with her son.

Leo watched them disappear into a room at the other end of the hall before closing the door and turning back to the laptop screen to find the team watching him with varying degrees of amusement. He resumed his seat and hoped the heat creeping up his neck didn't show.

Ian whistled. "She's pretty."

Harper playfully punched Ian in the arm. "Don't be such a guy."

"Hey, I am, though." Ian rubbed his arm with a grin.

"The child is adorable," Nina stated.

"Did you see his eyes?" Julianne asked. "So blue."

"Like his mother's," Tim said. "We have to get this guy who's threatening them."

"We will," Leo vowed. Affection for these folks expanded within his chest. The team had become his family. The only family he needed.

That he spent too many restless, sleepless nights

alone was of no consequence. The price he had to pay for his failures.

Max cleared his throat. "Leo, I trust you have the best interests of the witness and her family in mind at all times."

Leo straightened in his chair. A sudden rush of…not guilt, per se, but definitely something close, throbbed in his chest. There was no way Max could know the seeds of affection for Alicia and Charlie had burrowed deep within him. "Yes, sir. Always. What time should I expect to see you in the morning?"

"We'll leave at sunrise," Max replied.

"Okay, I'll call the police chief and let him know to expect us at the station midmorning."

"Righto." Max rose from his seat. "We'll see you soon, Leo. Go home, everyone. Get some rest. We have a lot of work ahead of us."

"Night, guys," Leo said before ending the video chat.

He placed the call to Chief Jarrett, letting the man know their plan for the morning. Leo then touched base with the forensic artist scheduled to arrive at the Settler's Valley police station by midmorning. Once they got a composite of the man who'd dumped the woman in the river, they would have a better chance of capturing him and putting an end to the threat hovering over Alicia.

And then Leo and the team could get on to the business of finding Jake. Leo prayed they wouldn't be too late to save his comrade's life.

Too keyed up to sleep, he gathered his night-vision goggles and kept watch out the bedroom window. True, on the other hand, had no problem falling asleep. The dog lay on the floor at the foot of the bed atop a folded blanket.

Ever since Jake had been abducted, Leo had had trouble resting. His mind kept replaying the events of that morning. The way the sunrise had broken over the horizon. The way Jake and his partner had had Leo's and True's backs. The hiss of the chemical gas filling the warehouse. Buddy's yelp as a bullet grazed his hind end. The *whomp-whomp* of the helicopter taking off. Jake's blood on the ground.

True suddenly jumped to his feet, emitting a low growl deep in his throat.

He searched the darkened night for whatever had spooked the dog. The moon shone high in the sky, its glow outlining the mountains in the distance. He searched the shadows for a threat. True let out a warning bark just as the faint strain of what sounded like a thousand hornets reached Leo's ears.

The drone was back.

Quickly he removed his assault rifle from its case and hurried out of the house with True at his side. Wearing his night-vision goggles, Leo could make out movement in the sky. The drone was coming from the east.

Hustling for the old Chevy truck to use as cover while he sighted the flying object through his scope, Leo vowed this time the unmanned aircraft was not going to escape.

Alicia lay on her bed surrounded by darkness, concentrating on calming her breathing. This day had not turned out as she'd expected. When she and Charlie had left for the river this morning, she'd wanted a nice relaxing time teaching her son to fish, and she'd hoped to be able to quell the growing restlessness she'd been feeling lately.

Instead, she'd witnessed a horrific crime and now the

lives of both her and her family were in danger. Night-marish images of the killer haunted her. The moment the woman's body hit the water looped through her mind like a scratch on a record. It took all her concentration to force herself to think of something else. *Someone* else.

Agent Leo Gallagher.

Charming and kind. Handsome and capable. Leo made her feel safe and cared for when she should be terrified. Like the mountain lions that roamed the Wyoming mountain range, the killer lurked, waiting for an opportunity to pounce. But she was confident Leo would protect them.

She couldn't deny her attraction to the tall and broad-shouldered FBI agent. She wasn't immune to his appeal. He made her heart race. And the caring way he handled Charlie made her insides melt.

But she was emotionally dead inside and had no intention of allowing any tender feelings to take root. Love had already led her down a perilous path to heartbreak, a place that was desolate and barren, to a pain she couldn't describe.

Better to keep her heart tucked away for eternity than to ever risk a repeat of that kind of hurt.

After learning of her husband's betrayals, she'd shut down, became numb. The only reason she hadn't shriveled up and turned to dust was because of Charlie. He needed her.

She'd thought Jeff had needed her as well but she'd been wrong.

So many years the fool.

Never again.

Her mind hummed with energy and her body vibrated with tension. She inhaled, filling her lungs, expanding her rib cage the way she'd been taught in her Pilates class, then slowly released her breath. The buzzing in her head intensified.

She sat up abruptly. The swift realization that the noise wasn't inside her skull but was outside the house trapped the air in her chest. For a moment she choked on fear.

The drone was back.

SEVEN

Not wanting to take the time to set up a proper shot, Leo steadied his elbows on the edge of the Chevy truck bed and sighted down the barrel of his assault rifle. He waited for the drone to pause for a split second, and then he took the shot. His bullet struck the drone dead-center.

The flying orb spun off course of its intended target. Several seconds later it exploded in a shower of sparks over the horse barn, lighting up the night sky like a Fourth of July peony firework. He didn't feel vindicated knowing the drone had indeed been rigged with explosives. Or that the man remotely piloting the drone decided to blow the thing instead of letting it crash to the ground.

But at least he'd kept the thing from reaching the Howard ranch house. He shuddered at the thought.

If he'd been off target or late in shooting the thing down...

Flames and debris rained down. Immediately, the dry timber of the wooden structure caught fire, and the flames licked at the roof, sending curling smoke heavenward, filling the air with a dusty haze.

Alarmed by the sight of the blaze, he grabbed his

cell phone from his pocket to call the fire department. True's bark could barely be heard over the snapping and popping of the burning barn.

The front porch light of the main house came on and he heard the door crash open. Alicia raced out wearing jeans, a hoodie sweatshirt and scuffed cowboy boots. Her dark hair cascaded over her shoulders. Adrenaline pumped through Leo as he dumped his rifle into the back bed of the old Chevy as she vaulted down the porch steps and ran toward the barn. He hurried to intercept her and snaked an arm around her waist, drawing her backward against his chest.

With a terrified yelp, her arms and legs splayed, her elbow smacked him in the chin. Pain reverberated through his head. The heel of her boot connected with his knee. His leg wobbled.

"Hey, hey. It's me—Leo," he rasped next to her ear.

She stilled then craned her neck to look at him. He could see the panic in her eyes. "The horses!"

He released her and thrust his cell phone into her hand. "Call 911. I'll get the horses."

Without waiting for her to protest, Leo ran to the barn. He stopped long enough to give True the command to wait. Leo didn't want the dog inside the burning building. True whined and barked.

"No," Leo said to the canine. "You stay."

The dog reluctantly sat but continued to bark, the pitch high with anxiety.

Smoke billowed in acrid puffs from beneath the barn door. Leo drew his black T-shirt up over his nose and mouth. He slid the door open and hit a wall of heat that bit into the exposed skin on his arms. He crouched and hurried inside.

Thankfully the fire was concentrated on the east wall and roof on the opposite side of the barn from the agitated horses, but that could change any moment if the stacks of hay bales caught a spark.

Blinking to ease the sting in his eyes from the intense smoke now ballooning through the barn, a precursor to the inferno that was eating its way toward the horses, he grabbed a nylon lead hanging on the wall beside the first stall.

"Come on, Stardust," he said to the scared horse. She whinnied and flicked her mane. Her hooves pawed at the stall door.

"Easy, now." He reached for her.

She shied away. Her wide eyes had a wild gleam to them, her nostrils flared and her heavy breaths came out in hot puffs.

Frustration pounded at his temples as his heart battered his rib cage. He didn't have time to train the horse to accept his touch. He needed to clip the lead onto the halter and get her out of the stall so he could rescue the other two horses.

"Let me." Soft hands took the nylon lead from his grasp.

Leo jerked around to find Alicia had followed him into the burning structure. She'd pulled the hood of her sweatshirt over her head to cover her hair and had her nose and mouth tucked inside her collar so that only her eyes were visible in the dancing light of the flames.

Fear for her safety ignited in his chest. "I've got this. You need to get out of here."

"*We* need to get the horses out of here," she countered in a calm voice that surprised him. "The fire department is on the way. So is Chief Jarrett. Dad's got

Charlie." She gripped his arm. "We'll open the paddock doors and get the horses outside then get them to the pasture away from the fire."

Seeing the logic in her words, Leo swiftly moved to collect the two remaining leads dangling on hooks by the stall doors, while Alicia slipped inside Stardust's stall and opened the back door to the paddock. Stardust ran for the fresh air.

Leo went to Apple's stall. The mare reared back. He held up a hand. "Whoa, girl. It's okay."

Behind the horse, Alicia opened the paddock door. Her slender dark silhouette filled the door frame. Spooked, Apple didn't turn and run the way Stardust had. Instead, she pushed toward the front of the stall, pawing at the inside door to get out. Leo blocked the mare, dodging a striking hoof. The only thing he could grab on to was Apple's ear.

For a brief second the horse stilled, allowing him to clip the lead in place. A loud whistle split the air. Apple's head jerked toward Alicia.

With a hand on Apple's shoulder and a firm grip on the lead, Leo maneuvered the horse out of the stall, managing to get stepped on only once, and into the paddock.

"Get them out of here," he shouted to Alicia. He inhaled smoke and coughed. His lungs burned as he hurried out of Apple's stall. He needed to get the final horse out. In the last stall, Brutus kicked at the door. This wouldn't be easy. Leo did an about-face, raced back through Apple's stall into the paddock and over to the door leading to Brutus's stall. He yanked the door wide.

The horse didn't need encouragement. Brutus charged out, head down, ears back. Leo jumped to the side but wasn't quick enough. The horse knocked into him, sending him flying.

He slammed against the paddock railing and his head cracked against the wood. Stars danced before his eyes.

Not stars.

Sparks.

Cinders.

Flames engulfed the barn, consuming the structure.

The shrill sound of sirens drew closer. Help arriving. It would be too late for the barn. But the firefighters would keep the blaze from jumping to the house.

Soft hands tugged at Leo. "Come on—you have to get up."

He staggered to his feet. True's panicked barking echoed inside his head. Gripping Alicia's arm, he urged her to move. His lungs were seared from the inside but he ignored the pain—his focus was on getting Alicia and the horses to safety.

The freaked-out animals ran in jagged paths around the paddock, looking for an escape. Dodging a frantic Brutus, the two of them made it to the back paddock gate that led to the pasture. He quickly unhooked the steel latch and pushed open the gate. Alicia whistled again, a sharp long blast that brought the horses' attention to her.

"Out!" she yelled. Brutus didn't hesitate. The horse bolted into the pasture, disappearing into the muted shadows of the landscape.

Stardust followed him. Apple ran back toward the barn as if seeking safety in her stall. Alicia whistled again and waved her arms, cutting her off.

Leo vaulted forward and snatched the lead that hung from Apple's halter and tugged her toward the open pasture gate. Once the mare made it safely into the pasture, he closed the gate, then turned to watch the barn collapse in an array of burning embers, dancing flames and coiling gray smoke.

"That was a huge explosion," Alicia gasped. "Did your bullet hitting the battery on the drone cause it to blow up?"

"No, lithium ion batteries don't do that," he told her grimly.

"Then why did it explode so spectacularly?"

He looked at her from the corner of his eye. "That thing was rigged with some type of explosive, either on a timer or triggered manually. Though I'm leaning more toward the latter."

He heard her breath hitch.

"You mean the house was the target?"

He kept silent, unwilling to voice his speculation.

"To silence me."

"I'm sorry about your barn."

"It's not your fault," she countered. "We saved the horses. They are all that matters. Everything else can be replaced."

He appreciated her pragmatic attitude. "I promised to keep you safe and I nearly failed. If not for True alerting me when he did..."

She slipped her hand into his. Her fingers were slender and strong as they wrapped around his. "You did save us. And praise God for that. If you hadn't shot down the drone, the house would be on fire." She squeezed his hand and looked up at him. The glow of the fire reflected in her eyes. What he saw there made his insides clench. "There's no telling if we'd have made it out alive."

She was looking at him like he was her hero. He

wasn't anyone's hero. Could never be a hero. Not the way she'd deserve. He wasn't a man to pin one's hopes on. He did his job then moved on to the next job. Getting emotionally involved on an assignment wasn't smart or practical.

He flexed his fingers, forcing her to release his hand. "Come on. We need to let everyone know we're okay."

Putting his hand to her lower back, he guided her around the burning barn. Harmon stood on the porch of the house with Charlie in his arms. True paced the length of the porch. Leo was thankful to see the dog safe and unharmed. A fire engine with hoses blasting a steady stream of water sat in the driveway. Men in turnout gear rushed forward to escort them out of the way.

Two paramedics hurried over. "Did you sustain any injuries?" one of them asked Leo.

"No, no. I'm fine," he assured the guy, trying to wave him off. "Just check Ms. Duncan out."

"You have some burns," the paramedic insisted. Leo let the man look at his singed arms as he kept his gaze trained on Alicia. The other paramedic listened to her lungs and shone a light in her eyes. Leo never would have forgiven himself if she'd been seriously hurt.

"Mommy!" Charlie's exuberant cry carried over the noise of the fire hoses and the dying blaze that had destroyed the barn. Harmon hung on to the boy as Alicia broke away from the paramedic to be reunited with her child.

Leo addressed the paramedic who had examined her. "Is she okay?"

"Yes," he said. "No sign of burns or smoke inhalation."

Relief flooded through him.

True let out a loud, joyous bark and jumped from the porch, landing on all fours at a run. Leo went down on one knee to catch True as the dog leaped into his arms and licked his face. "I'm glad to see you, too," Leo told the dog.

After a moment, Leo rose, got an okay from the paramedic and headed toward where Chief Jarrett stood talking to his officers.

"Chief," Leo said as he came to a stop.

"Agent Gallagher, it's good to see you unharmed. I understand you saved the horses," Jarrett stated. He was dressed in civilian clothes. Wranglers, snakeskin boots and a plaid button-down. His silver hair was hidden beneath a Stetson. Apparently he'd been off-duty when he'd received the call about the fire.

"Wasn't all me," Leo replied, his gaze going to Alicia. She held Charlie tight to her chest. Her clothes were sooty and her face was smeared with specks of black ash, but he was awestruck by her beauty. A warrior princess willing to risk her life for her animals and her family. A woman to admire and respect. A woman who would love with the same intensity.

Something Leo would never experience. The thought left him hollow inside.

Jarrett followed his gaze. "She's quite special. I'd hate to see her hurt."

Leo's gaze snapped back to the police chief. Sensing the older man wasn't just referring to the physical danger threatening Alicia's life, he stated firmly, "You don't have to worry. I will do everything in my power to protect her."

Even from himself.

Alicia tiptoed out of Charlie's room. He'd finally fallen back to sleep. It had taken a great deal of coaxing to get him to settle down after the chaos of the barn fire. Her own heart still beat too fast with adrenaline and fear. She didn't explain to him the true nature of the blaze. Her three-year-old son didn't need to know that Leo had shot down a drone armed with explosives that was intent on eliminating her as a witness to a horrible crime.

Dad and Leo were still outside assessing the damage to the barn. True stayed close to his handler. She hurried to the downstairs front window. The last of the firefighters drove away, but Chief Jarrett had left a patrol car with two officers to keep watch.

She sent up a prayer of gratitude for the presence of Leo and True. Without the agent and his dog, she and her family would be toast. Literally.

She left the house to join the men. Leo kept his gaze on the dark horizon, no doubt assessing for any sort of threat. True sniffed the air, his nose twitching.

Dad put his hand on her shoulder. The wrinkles in his face were deeper and his eyes troubled. He'd misbuttoned his shirt, attesting to the fact he'd dressed in a hurry to see what was going on outside. "Thank the good Lord above you brought Leo home with you."

Alicia smiled, remembering how Dad had greeted the agent earlier in the day. A shotgun welcome. "I agree. He and True are a blessing." She was aware of Leo's quick glance.

"I'll say good-night now," Dad said. "Hopefully there won't be any more excitement tonight…er, this morning."

For a moment she and Leo were silent as they watched her dad stride slowly back to the house.

Once he was inside, she asked, "What if the guy has another drone?"

Leo turned toward her. His face was streaked with black soot and there were singe marks on his clothes and red, irritated skin on his exposed arms. "True will alert us again." He gestured to the officers in their car. "We have reinforcements now."

Touching a gentle hand to his sleeve, she said, "Did the paramedics look at your burns?"

He glanced down at her hand then back to her face. "They're superficial heat burns, Alicia. Thankfully, I never made contact with a flame. The medic gave me some antibiotic ointment to use."

"We should get you inside and tend to your wounds," she insisted. He'd suffered the burns saving her horses. The least she could do was dress his injuries.

"I'll deal with them later," Leo replied gruffly. "You should get some rest. Tomorrow the forensic artist will be here to work with you. And my boss and another agent are coming to town."

"They are welcome to stay here as well," she told him. "We have one more guest room and Charlie can bunk with me so one of them can use his room."

A soft smiled touched his lips. "That's very generous of you. I'll let my boss know. That would mean two more dogs in your house. Are you up for that?"

Having True in the house gave her an added measure of comfort. Two more highly trained canines would only increase the level of security. "Of course." She captured his hand, liking the feel of his calloused palm against hers and his strong fingers linking through her own. "I won't be able to rest until I know you've taken care of your burns."

He stared at her for a long moment. She held his gaze, afraid he'd withdraw his hand the way he had earlier. She wasn't sure what had made him retreat from her. And she shouldn't want to comfort him, shouldn't want to be so close to him, but everything inside of her demanded that she take care of him. After all, he'd risked his life to save her family and had saved her horses.

He was simply doing his job, she reminded herself. He wasn't here because he cared about her. Mistaking his bravery and courage for something more, something personal, would be foolish. She couldn't allow herself to form a false attachment. Her heart was battered and bruised enough. Her gaze dropped to her boots.

Fatigue drained the last of her energy and she slipped her hand from his. "You're right—I need to rest," she said but couldn't help adding, "Please promise me you'll take care of your arms."

He inclined his head. "I promise."

Suspecting he was the sort of man who kept his promises, her heart folded in on itself.

The next morning arrived far too early for Alicia. She watched the smoke-stained sky pinken with the dawn, not having slept much at all. Yesterday had been overwhelming. First the man dumping the woman's body in the river, then being shot at, then the fire.

She forced herself to rise and start the day. She needed to be awake and ready to give a detailed description of the killer to the forensic artist. She knew she'd have no trouble recalling the man's face. His image haunted her mind.

After a quick shower, she put on her favorite jeans

and a floral-print top that she knew looked good on her—not that she was dressing to impress.

Okay, well, maybe a bit. She wanted Leo to think she was pretty, especially after how awful she'd looked once they'd dealt with the horses last night.

Wanting him to find her attractive was totally ridiculous. Deep down she knew that. Especially considering how she usually didn't have an issue with vanity.

During her marriage, Jeff had preferred she wear dresses and makeup. He'd liked to joke she was his arm candy. Little had she known he had more sweets to choose from than Willy Wonka.

When she'd moved home, she'd overhauled her closet and thrown out every last dress she'd owned and all but a few essential items of makeup.

Never again would she be defined by her wrapper.

It didn't matter what she looked like. Her son loved her whether she had on fancy clothes or barn duds. Charlie's opinion of her was the only one that mattered. Not the ruggedly handsome agent's.

Still, there was a part of her that wanted to apply a touch of mascara and lip gloss.

Irritated with herself, she refrained from opening her makeup bag and headed out of her room. Leo and Charlie sat at the dining-room table with Dad and the remnants of a pancake breakfast pushed aside to make room for the game I Spy. True sat nearby, with tail wagging.

Charlie chatted away merrily and Leo's focus was totally on him. Alicia's heart exalted to see their two heads bent close together as they worked on connecting the pictures on the large puzzle-like pieces in the matching game.

She couldn't begin to express how grateful she was

to Leo for keeping his promise to play the game with her son. The unexpected burn of tears pricked the backs of her eyes and she quickly blinked them away. She met her father's gaze. He nodded with a smile as if sensing how choked up she was over this man's kindness to her child.

Leo glanced up and saw her. He gave her a lopsided grin that did funny things to her insides. "Good morning."

"Morning," she said as she headed to the kitchen for a cup of coffee.

"There's a stack of pancakes in the oven," her dad told her.

"Thanks, Dad," she said. "That's a nice surprise."

Dad's mouth quirked. "Don't thank me. Agent Leo did the honors."

Her gaze darted to Leo. "You made breakfast?"

His grin broadened. "I can cook. I figured it was the least I could do in return for putting me up."

She wrapped her hands around her mug. "You're our guest. I should have been up earlier to feed you."

"You needed your rest," he replied warmly. "Besides, this gave Charlie and me a chance to play. He's beating me, by the way." He winked.

She chuckled, liking this playful side to him. There was something about this man that called to her in an elemental way she hadn't experienced before. With Jeff, their romance had started in high school. She'd been the tomboy most of the guys thought of as a sister until the Duncans moved to town. Jeff had pursued her from the moment they met. She'd been blown away by the attention and his charm. He'd had such a big personality and had promised her the world. But what she'd ended up with were lies and betrayals.

She turned away from the sight of her beautiful son and the handsome agent to fix a plate of pancakes and told herself not to get used to Leo being here. He would be leaving soon.

Once the killer was caught and she was no longer in danger. Then life could go back to normal.

She wanted a quiet, simple life. She wanted to raise her son and in time go back to teaching. She wasn't looking for anything more.

Especially with a man who kept his promises. A man who would be dangerous to her heart.

EIGHT

"Is this him?" Brian Ames, the forensic artist, held up the sketch of the man Alicia had spent the past hour describing.

They were seated in an interrogation room at the Settler's Valley police department. Brian had said the sterile, windowless room would be less distracting for her as she recalled the details of the killer. He was right.

Alicia squirmed in the hard plastic chair. An involuntary shudder worked its way over her limbs. Fear swirled around her like a dark cloud and her mouth went dry. The sketch artist was good at his job, producing an amazingly realistic rendition of the man she'd seen in the boat who'd dumped the woman's body into the river.

She made herself take in the angular chin, the hawk-like nose, the piercing, close-set eyes and tightly cropped hair. She would know this man at a glance. She'd seen him on the river and then through the rearview mirror as he chased her in the stolen truck. She'd been right to think he would haunt her for a very long time. "Yes. That's him."

Brian handed the photo to Leo. He and True had taken a position behind her by the door to quietly observe.

Dad and Charlie were still at the ranch with four armed officers in place for protection while fire investigators combed through the debris left by the exploding drone.

Leo's big hand came to rest on her shoulder. His touch comforted and soothed. "You did good."

Pleased by his approval, she glanced up at him. "What happens now?"

"We make copies of the sketch and put it into the hands of every officer and law-enforcement agency around the county. We'll also run the image through facial recognition and pray we can identify him."

"Do you think he's still in town?" After last night's failed attempt to eliminate her with an exploding drone, she prayed the man had given up and fled. A pipe dream, she knew, but still…it couldn't hurt to hope.

"He seems pretty determined," Leo replied, effectively dimming her fledgling optimism. "But with this…" He held up the drawing. "We'll capture him."

Though she appreciated his confidence, a chill skated across her flesh. Averting her gaze from the image on the paper, she murmured, "From your lips to God's ears."

A knock had Leo moving from her side to open the door. A young officer stood there.

"Agent Gallagher, Chief Jarrett wanted me to let you know your boss has arrived."

"Thank you, Officer," Leo said then turned back to her and held out his hand. "Come on—I'd like to introduce you to Special Agent West."

She rose and slipped her hand into his and was startled by how natural and right it felt to have their palms fitting together so perfectly, as if they'd had this connection between them forever. It was a strange sensation to realize how much she'd come to admire and respect this man so quickly.

Was she crazy? Were her feelings born from the trauma of the past twenty-four hours? Had to be. She knew very little about Agent Gallagher. Though she wished she knew more. She thought back to their time in the barn and about how uncomfortable he'd seemed when she'd asked him about his life and if he'd ever come close to marriage. She'd sensed something bad had happened to him. Had he lost a loved one?

She expected Leo to let go of her hand once they were in the hallway, but instead, his strong and capable fingers curled around hers, keeping her tethered to him as they headed for the chief's office. True, nails clicking rhythmically on the linoleum floor, walked on Leo's other side.

Disconcerted by the pleasant glow infusing her, she wanted to deny how nice it was to hold Leo's much larger hand, to have someone want to touch her and be with her. Not that she would make the mistake of thinking he had feelings for her beyond the constraints of his job. He didn't. He'd already been clear that his job was to protect her and her family, nothing more.

Still, it had been so long since the yearning for companionship, except for that of her son and father, had gripped her in its tenacious hold. She'd thought she was doing okay without a man in her life. But now she wondered if the restlessness she'd been battling lately stemmed from loneliness.

Two people stood with the chief outside his office door. The chief, dressed in his light beige police uniform, looked relaxed as he talked to a man and a woman, both of whom wore dark uniforms similar to the one Leo wore with the FBI logo splashed across their backs. The woman carried a laptop case draped across her body.

Two very different dogs sat at attention next to their handlers. As they approached, both dogs turned to stare at them, alerting their handlers to her and Leo's presence.

"Ah, here they are," Chief Jarrett said with a smile.

The woman's gaze dropped to Alicia and Leo's joined hands and she arched an eyebrow. Suddenly self-conscious and feeling a bit embarrassed by the contact, Alicia flexed her fingers and Leo slipped his hand from hers.

Addressing the male agent, Leo said, "Max, this is Alicia Duncan." He touched a hand to the small of her back, the pressure warm and pleasant. "Alicia, this is special agent in charge Max West and his K-9 partner, Opal."

The tall, muscular man smiled, though his eyes assessed her with intense scrutiny. A scar ran down one side of his face, making her think of a pirate. "Ms. Duncan, it's nice to meet you." He held out his hand.

"Likewise, Agent West," she said and briefly shook his hand. Gesturing to the dog sitting beside him, she asked, "Is she a boxer?"

The dog's ears perked up. Max touched Opal's head. She had a brown coat with a white chest and paws. "Yes. Her specialty is explosives detection."

They could have used her last night. But True had done his job and alerted them to the threat. Leo had done the rest. Together, the K-9 team had saved the lives of her and her family. She'd be forever grateful.

"This is Agent Julianne Martinez and her K-9 partner, Thunder," Leo said, indicating the attractive woman standing next to his boss. She had dark hair pulled back into a low ponytail and clear, olive skin. The brown, black and white foxhound lifted a paw as if wanting to shake Alicia's hand.

Unsure if she should touch the dog, Alicia kept her hands at her sides. "Hello, Agent Martinez and Thunder."

Julianne's smile was warm as she reached out to clasp Alicia's hand. "How are you holding up?"

Slightly taken aback by the other woman's compassion, Alicia answered honestly, "I'm not sure."

"She's doing great," Leo interjected. "She's handling all of this in stride."

Pleased by his words, Alicia stared at him. Obviously, he didn't know how freaked out she was by all that had taken place in the past twenty-four hours. Or how close to the edge she'd been after Jeff's death, when the world as she'd known it had unraveled.

Through her prayers she felt the Lord's presence as she made the decision to move home to Settler's Valley and live with her father. Her faith and her family had saved her from spiraling down a dark hole. Picking up the pieces of her heart had been hard. Learning to trust a man again was even harder. Yet in such a short time Leo had earned a measure of trust she hadn't thought she'd ever give again.

"Alicia, how did it go with the forensic artist?" the chief asked.

"Better than I expected," she replied, tucking her hands into the pockets of her lightweight, zippered jacket.

Leo held out the sketched image of the killer. "Here's the perpetrator's likeness."

Julianne took the paper from his hand. "I'll send a copy to Dylan. If this guy is in any database in the world, Dylan will find him."

Alicia looked at Leo. "Dylan?"

"Our unit's communications tech," Leo replied. "He's the best at what he does."

"I'd like to make copies to give to my officers," the chief interjected.

"Show me to your copier," Julianne said.

The chief led the female agent and her partner away.

"Any more information on Jake?" Leo asked his boss.

Max scrubbed a hand over his jaw. "No. I have every law-enforcement agency in the state of Wyoming on the lookout for anyone resembling him."

Leo's frustration was easy to see. His jaw tightened and he rubbed the back of his neck. Leo had mentioned his fellow agent had been abducted. She wondered what had happened.

"How do we know the anonymous tip is even valid?" Leo asked tersely.

Max shrugged. "We don't. There have been tons of calls with sightings of Jake since the news went public that we captured Reginald and that Jake was missing, presumed kidnapped by the Duprees. Our job is to follow every lead in hopes one will eventually pan out. Though this one… There was something different about it."

"Yeah, I get it," Leo replied in a tone fraught with frustration. "We can use the publicity to help find Jake."

"That's the hope," Max replied.

Leo turned his gaze on her. "We normally keep our missions under wrap and out of the public eye."

She imagined that would be hard with the dogs and all. But she'd seen Leo and True in action. They excelled at their jobs. She had no doubt all the agents and their partners were excellent officers of the law and stealthy when needed.

Leo blew out a breath, then said to Max, "Alicia has offered for you and Julianne to stay out at the ranch."

Max met her gaze. "That's very hospitable of you."

"I figure with three human agents and three canines, we'd be extra safe," she replied with a smile.

He nodded. "Good thinking. If you're sure, we'll accept."

"I'm sure." She liked the idea of extra protection. In addition, they'd be a buffer between her and Leo. And Charlie would have two new people to interact with, which might divert some of his hero-worship attention from Leo. The last thing she wanted was her son becoming too emotionally attached to the dashing agent.

Julianne and the chief returned with a stack of duplicated copies of the killer's image.

"Is there an office or conference room we could use?" Max asked the chief.

"Of course." He showed them to a small conference room with a square table and several mismatched chairs. He held up the copies of the killer's image in his hands. "I'm going to distribute these now."

Max gestured to the open door of the conference room. "Ladies, after you."

Surprised by the invitation, Alicia walked into the room and took a seat at the table. The others followed. When they were all situated, Julianne fired up her laptop. Within a few moments, the screen was filled with the live video feed of the face of a blond-haired young man wearing a set of black horn-rimmed glasses and a loud print shirt.

"Dylan, did you get the picture I faxed over?" Julianne asked.

"I did and I'm searching cyberspace for a match,"

Dylan said. He peered at Alicia. "Hello. You must be Ms. Duncan. I'm Dylan O'Leary."

She hesitated a moment, tempted to revert to her maiden name. But Charlie was a Duncan and for him she'd remain one, too. "I am. It's nice to meet you, Dylan."

He flashed a brief smile. "I'm sure it's not but I appreciate the sentiment."

Alicia couldn't help but like the affable young man. "I'll admit I wish I were meeting all of you under different circumstances." Her gaze met Leo's.

After a heartbeat, he turned to the computer screen. "Dylan, do you have an ID on the victim?"

"I do. Her name was Virginia Carter from Reno, Nevada. According to her family, she was on a road trip visiting college friends. They hadn't heard from her in a few days and had already alerted the authorities."

Alicia's heart hurt for Virginia's family. Suffering a loss was never easy, but to have the death be at the hands of someone else made it worse. When Jeff was killed in the line of duty, his murderer had been caught, convicted and sentenced to life in prison. There was some comfort in that. Alicia sent up a prayer they would find Virginia's murderer and give the family closure.

"Do we know where she was staying?" Julianne asked. "We might find a clue as to how she crossed paths with the killer."

Dylan's fingers rapped against his keyboard. "Her credit card was used at a resort in Burns Junction."

"Grizzly Lodge," Alicia supplied. "It's a luxury hotel at the top of the Blackthorn Mountain range north of here, where the mouth of the river begins."

"Julianne and I will go to Burns Junction," Max

stated. "We'll check out Virginia Carter's hotel room and look for her car."

"And search for Jake," Julianne added. "If the killer thought Esme Dupree was in Burns Junction, then maybe…?" She shrugged with a grimace.

"Do we know where in Wyoming the marshals have Esme stashed?" Leo asked. "That might be good to know so we can plan on helping with Esme's protection."

"They wouldn't give out details," Max said. "After their marshal slipped up and revealed that Esme was in Wyoming to the man posing as me, they've been tight-lipped. I don't blame them. That mistake could cost her her life and us the case."

"Do we think the killer went after Virginia by mistake?" Dylan asked.

Leo tugged at his earlobe. "I think his job was to silence Esme and he found Virginia. She matches Esme's description to a T. If I hadn't seen Esme up close I would have thought they were one and the same."

"The message was meant to scare Esme out of hiding," Julianne said. "Do we believe this guy—" she held up the sketched image of the man who'd put a target on Alicia "—is the only thug Angus Dupree has out searching for Esme?"

There was a moment of silence. The tension in the room grew tenfold.

Finally, Max said, "Angus Dupree will stop at nothing to silence his niece. One thug? No. Dupree has an army out looking for Esme."

Alicia's mouth went dry. She swallowed hard, then said, "Then there could be more victims who look like Esme."

All eyes turned to her. She held Leo's gaze.

He gave her a grim nod. "Yes, there could be more."

"Dylan, have there been any other missing persons filed?" Max asked. "Or victims found within the state of Wyoming?"

"Let me search." The communications tech's fingers flew over the keyboard. His face paled. "Three women with similar descriptions matching Esme Dupree have been reported missing. One from Casper, a nurse who hasn't shown up for work in a few days, and another woman, a librarian, from Cheyenne. Both of those women went missing on the same day."

Alicia shivered. Worry for the missing women and for the agents who were working to find them bubbled in her tummy. Though she understood the dangers of a career in law enforcement, being this close to it all made her anxious. She lifted up a silent prayer of protection for the agents. And a prayer the women would be found.

"More than one perp," Max confirmed. "I'll need to let the US Marshals Service know."

"And the third?" Julianne prompted.

"A hairstylist, Sue Ellen Bishop, from a township named Drytown," Dylan said. "She missed her appointments yesterday afternoon and this morning."

"That's not far from here." She widened her eyes in alarm. "Upriver, about twenty miles. If he took her from Drytown, he could have dumped her body anywhere along the river."

"Seems our guy is following the Blackthorn River," Leo stated. "Or was, until you saw him."

She swallowed back the terror clawing up her throat. "As much as I hate having my life threatened, if spotting him stops him, then so be it. I have all of you to protect me." And God watching over her.

Leo's expression softened with gratitude. "Thank you for your confidence in us."

The weight of Max's and Julianne's stares made her tear her gaze away from Leo. Heat crept up her neck and into her cheeks. Until she knew for sure what was prompting her attraction to Agent Gallagher—his kindness, his willingness to put himself in harm's way for her and her family, or her own aching loneliness—she wasn't about to be caught mooning over him like a lovesick teenager.

"True and I need to get on the river ASAP," Leo stated. "I'll get the diver back here. In the meantime, I'll ask Chief Jarrett to have an escort for Alicia back to the ranch."

Her gaze jerked back to him. "No. I'm coming with you to the river. I know this area well. Up and down both sides of the shore. As kids, my friends and I spent every day playing along the Blackthorn during the summer."

"I can't allow it," Leo stated flatly.

She arched an eyebrow. "*Allow* it? Excuse me, Agent Gallagher, but you have no say in what I do."

"It's for your own protection."

Her hackles rose. "Are you saying you can't handle protecting me away from the ranch?"

"That's not what I'm saying," he said through clenched teeth. "But out in the field there are too many unknowns. Variables I can't control."

"That woman is out there. We are her only chance of being found." Preferably alive. But she wasn't naive enough to hold on to that hope.

"Not we—*me*."

"Are you always so arrogant?" She sliced the air with

her hand. "I'm not some helpless sap. You need a guide. We're wasting time debating this."

Leo opened his mouth to argue but Max stepped forward. "Gallagher, a word."

Leo looked ready to argue with his boss but pressed his lips together and stepped out of the conference room. When the two men were gone, Alicia bit her lip. "I hope I didn't get him in trouble."

Julianne smiled kindly. "Don't worry—you didn't. Leo's a bit of a control freak. He feels bad about Jake. Not that he could have done anything differently. It could have easily been him they abducted."

"He'd mentioned a fellow agent was kidnapped but I didn't know that last part."

Julianne grimaced. "Leo feels like he should have somehow kept Jake from being taken. We all feel that way but Leo more so because he and Jake were together on the ground of the warehouse."

Now Leo's hypervigilance made sense. He felt responsible for his friend's abduction. And was afraid he'd fail to protect her as well. She hurt for him. It couldn't be easy to carry so much weight on his shoulders. She was another burden for him to bear.

She understood his reluctance to take her with him. Really, she did. But he had to understand that she wasn't one to sit idle when there was something she could do to help.

Finding Sue Ellen Bishop from Drytown gave Alicia a purpose. A way to take back some power from the maniac determined to kill again.

NINE

"What's going on, Gallagher?" Max asked once he and Leo were in the hallway. True sat at Leo's side while Opal lay on the floor at Max's feet.

Leo ran a hand through his hair as embarrassment flooded his system. He'd just argued with a civilian in front of his boss and coworker. *So not cool.*

There was just something about Alicia that made him overly sensitive and heightened his need to keep control of the situation. He wanted to put her in a glass case and keep her there until this madman was caught.

He'd never felt so protective of a civilian involved in one of their cases before. Why Alicia? He didn't really know her. Did his feelings for her have something to do with Jake's kidnapping? That had to be why. But he couldn't tell his boss. His pride wouldn't allow it.

"I don't know," he finally muttered. "I don't like the idea of taking her into the field. There's too much risk involved."

Max dropped his chin. "No more risk than her staying at the ranch. If she's with you then you can protect her. That is what you want, right? I can have Julianne take over the protection detail, if you'd prefer."

"No," he replied quickly. Too quickly if Max's arched eyebrow was any indication. Leo took a deep breath. "I'll take her with me."

The other man nodded. "I'm sure Chief Jarrett will supply a couple of uniforms to accompany you."

"That would work," Leo said. Though he'd keep Alicia within arm's length, having the backup would be welcomed.

Max's cell phone rang. He fished the device from the breast pocket of his uniform. "West."

He listened a moment, his expression darkening. "Understood. Thank you for letting me know." He clicked off. "The US Marshals were moving Esme to a new locale when they were ambushed. One marshal was shot but is expected to live. The other marshal managed to escape with Esme unharmed."

Leo's gut twisted with both alarm and relief. "That was close."

"Too close. The marshals are looking within their ranks to see if they have a leak."

"They may not have one," Leo said. "If Dupree has goons all over the state looking for Esme, one could have ferreted her out. Once the marshals have her relocated, Dupree will have to call off his thugs." At least Leo hoped so. The United States was a big place, and without a general location for Esme, there was no way Dupree could hope to find her. But he had a feeling that the guy after Alicia wouldn't stop until he'd accomplished his goal—to silence the witness.

With True on leash, Leo and Alicia made their way through the dense woods along the Blackthorn River, accompanied by two of Settler's Valley's finest. With every snap of a twig or rustle of a branch, Leo's senses jumped. He knew he was being overly cautious but was there such a thing when it came to the safety of a civilian and not just any civilian. Alicia was more than a mere witness; she was a good mother and caregiver to her father. She had a big heart and deep wounds, yet she also had a spine of steel and a feisty spirit that he respected and admired. He was definitely losing perspective where she was concerned. He could feel himself slipping like loose gravel down a steep slope.

The crashing rush of the swift-moving river reached them through the trees, the water unseen behind the matted foliage. They'd parked at the marina and hiked from there, passing the place where Alicia had seen Virginia Carter go into the water. As they'd reached the canyon, Leo was sure they'd have to turn back and drive around the high cliffs, but Alicia had shown them a barely discernible trail that led up and over the rock formation. Now they were on the other side of the canyon where the cottonwoods and aspen trees towered over smaller trees and shrubs.

Leo caught glimpses of the river through the heavy branches. "Can we get to the shoreline?" True needed to be closer to the water to pick up on a scent.

"We will once we get past this thicket," Alicia assured him, picking her way through the massive tangles of branches and leaves. "The county really needs to do something about this mess. These Russian olive trees are so invasive. And the salt cedar is a noxious weed that's choking out the natural plants. I've heard up in the Big Horn area the plants are being removed." She glanced back at him. "Sorry, I'm sure you're not interested in our local environmental troubles."

A twig stuck out of her dark hair and the sunlight filtering through the canopy of branches overhead kissed her pink cheeks. She was really lovely. He gave her a smile. "The environment affects us all. It's nice that you care so much."

She returned his smile and his heart thumped against his rib cage. There was no rational way of blaming his response to her on an underlying need to make up for failing to protect Jake. He was attracted to her, pure and simple. The realization nearly made him stumble. Leo had no idea what to do with this knowledge. He wouldn't act on it. His only course of action was to ignore his growing feelings for the lovely widow and hope he survived this mission with his heart intact.

True barked and strained at his leash, diverting Leo's attention away from Alicia. "He smells something." To the canine, he said, "Find it." He let go of the leash. True dashed through the brush. Leo grabbed Alicia's hand. "Come on."

Together they fought their way through the thicket with the two police officers right behind them. They found True five feet away at the water's edge.

A jumbled mass of broken tree branches and debris created a platform for True to stand on. He paced back and forth, his bark echoing across the river. He'd definitely caught a scent. The dog stopped barking when he saw Leo, but he kept pacing, his paws sure on the waterlogged wood.

Leo stopped a few feet away and squeezed Alicia's hand. "Stay here."

She'd gone pale. "Did he find Sue Ellen?"

"I don't know yet," he told her. He wouldn't know until the diver could get in the water.

She clutched his arm. "Did you hear that?"

Leo stilled, listening. He heard the rush of the river, the wind in the trees. "What?"

Her nose scrunched up. "I'm not sure. It sounded like a whine."

"It could have been True," he said. "He wants to go into the water."

She nodded and released her hold on him. Leo carefully made his way to the river's edge, noting footprints in the moist earth along with grooves in the dirt as if something had been dragged into the water. A bad feeling churned in his gut. He didn't believe things were going to turn out well for Sue Ellen Bishop. *Please, let me be wrong, Lord.*

He gestured to one of the officers. "Call for a forensic team. Give them our location and tell them we need a diver ASAP."

"Yes, sir," the young officer said, taking his cell phone from his pocket.

The other officer took out a small digital camera from his utility belt and took pictures of the footprints and drag marks.

Leo moved slowly, conscientious not to damage the evidence, and joined True on the debris. He peered into the murky river and sucked in a sharp breath. Tangled in the branches and sticks he could discern the unmistakable outline of a female body, weighted down below the surface, where the water wasn't as deep as in the middle of the canyon.

Sickened to have found another dead woman, Leo turned away. He wanted to be mad at God but this wasn't His fault. A human man made the choice to kill.

He was responsible, and Leo would make sure he spent many years in prison for his crimes.

Grateful that Alicia's view of the corpse was blocked by the debris, he glanced toward where she'd been standing to find her gone.

His heart stalled out. Panic rushed in, the blood draining from his face. His heart cramped with dread. He'd only turned his back on her for a second. But he knew that was all it took. A moment of inattention and a life could end.

No! He wouldn't let that happen to Alicia. He couldn't let another person he cared about die on his watch. He had to find her.

"Alicia!"

Hearing Leo's frantic call, Alicia yelled, "Here! I'm over here."

She knelt down and peered into the thick bushes. A young, yellow Labrador stared back at her with dark, frightened eyes. She'd known she'd heard a whining noise and had feared she'd find a child. She hadn't been able to ignore the sound of distress, so she'd gone searching for the source. At the sound of Leo's panic she realized she'd acted impulsively, rashly. Shame washed over her. She'd been careless and upset him needlessly.

Behind her, Leo crashed through the underbrush with True at his heels and both skidded to a halt. "Are you hurt? What happened? Why did you disappear?"

Glancing over her shoulder, she grimaced at how visibly shaken he was. Guilt knotted her stomach. "I'm sorry. I shouldn't have left. I heard that noise again and followed it to this bush." She pointed. "There's a puppy in here."

Leo scrubbed a hand over his face and growled, "You nearly gave me a heart attack. Don't ever do that again."

Instead of becoming defensive at his words, as she normally would, she strove to soothe his ire. She deserved his anger and for some reason it made her feel cared for. "I didn't mean to scare you. I truly am sorry."

He blew out a breath and seemed to gather his composure before he nodded then knelt down beside her to look at the pup. True sat perfectly still, his intelligent eyes observing them. "Hey there, little fellow."

The puppy shrank back even more.

"What should we do?" Alicia hated the idea of the puppy out in the woods all alone.

Leo dug out a handful of treats from a pocket in his pants. He laid one down on the ground just out of the pup's reach. "It looks like he's wearing a collar. Hopefully we can contact his owner."

The pup sniffed the air, then put his nose to the ground and scuttled forward an inch, then another until he could stretch his mouth to gobble up the treat. Leo laid down another treat a little farther from the bush and backed up, giving the puppy space. True rose but made no move toward the younger dog or the treat.

Alicia scooted back alongside of Leo, marveling at his ingenuity and his canine partner's restraint. But then again, he was a trained K-9 handler with a highly trained K-9 officer.

When the pup ventured farther out to grab the next treat, Leo put out his hand with a treat in the center of his palm.

Nervous he'd be bitten, she asked, "Should you do that?"

He shrugged. "He'll either take my offer or he'll back away."

The little Lab went down onto his belly and shuffled forward to extend his muzzle as far as he could to take the treat from Leo's hand.

"Good boy," Leo cooed. From another pocket he brought out a shorter leash and swiftly hooked it to the puppy's collar. Then he gave him another treat.

"Wow, that was fast," she said. She doubted she'd have been able to coax the dog out from beneath the bushes so easily, even if she'd had treats in her pocket.

One of the officers approached. "Sir, the forensic team is here. They came by boat."

Leo nodded. "We'll be right there."

Alicia's stomach dropped. "True found her, didn't he?"

His expression turned grim. "He found someone. We won't know if it's Sue Ellen Bishop until we can get a positive ID."

He handed Alicia a handful of treats and the leash. "Here, you take him while I talk to the forensic team."

Stunned, she shook her head. "I don't know anything about dogs."

"He's a puppy." Leo smiled at the young dog sitting so patiently watching them. "He's been well trained. I'd say he's at least four months old."

"Okay, great, but what do I do?"

"Hold the treats like this in your hand." He demonstrated cupping several treats in his palm and holding them in place with his thumb. "That way he has to use his nose to find them and then his tongue to get them rather than his teeth. Keeps the fingers safe."

She did as he instructed.

"Good. Start walking. If he follows, give him a treat.

If he doesn't want to follow, coax him with a treat," Leo told her briskly. He was clearly anxious to get back to the river.

Determined to get through this, she took a step and said, "Come."

The puppy immediately obeyed. Pleasantly surprised, she offered him a treat. He gladly accepted from her cupped hand. Holding the leash, she and the pup followed Leo and True back to the river, where a Settler's Valley police boat had come ashore several feet away from where True still stood atop the pile of broken tree stumps and branches. Alicia couldn't see what had True so agitated and she was thankful.

She squatted down next to the puppy. Gingerly, so as not to frighten him more, she reached out to stroke his chest. He leaned into her, obviously enjoying the rub. She glanced at the little blue bone-shaped dog tag hanging from his collar. His name was River and he belonged to Sue Ellen Bishop. Her heart sank. Poor baby had lost his owner.

An hour later, they pulled the latest victim from the river. Unwilling to have the visual in her head, she turned away, just as she had when they'd pulled Virginia Carter's body from the water. It was bad enough living with the killer's face imprinted on her brain. Seeing his lifeless victims would be too much.

The crack of a gun firing split the air. Something passed close to Alicia's head. Less than a second later, Leo wrapped his arms around her and took her to the ground, covering her with his big body. For a shocked second, her mind refused to process what was happening.

Leo's weight pressing her down made it difficult

to breathe. His aftershave competed with the pungent smell of the earth beneath her. His body shielded her from the flying bullets. A comfort, yet a stark reminder of the danger they were in.

"Keep your head down." His urgent whisper penetrated through the stunned haze clouding her thoughts.

Someone had shot at her. Again.

True's barking filled her ears.

"Down!" Leo commanded.

True flattened onto his belly, though his ears remained up and a snarl bared his teeth, showing his upset at the threat.

The puppy whined and strained at the leash attached to his collar, clearly frightened by the sound and the humans' actions.

The two police officers withdrew their sidearms and took positions behind trees. The forensic team scattered, finding places to hide.

"We're going to find cover," Leo told her. "On three, we belly-crawl to that cottonwood."

She followed the line of his finger to a large tree about four feet away. Belly-crawl. The words reverberated through her head. Images of war and soldiers crawling beneath barbed wire flickered through her mind, giving her courage and strength. She was in a war for her life. She had to survive for her son's sake. "One."

"That's it," Leo murmured, approval and reassurance oozing from his tone. "Two." He took a breath. "Three."

Leo scrambled off of her, allowing her to move by. She stayed low, digging her elbows into the ground and pushing forward with her knees. She tugged the puppy with her. Another bullet hit the ground near her hip. Bits of dirt peppered her side. Flinching, she sped up her crawl until she was safe behind the tree, then gathered the puppy into her arms. Leo and True were quick to follow. In sync with each other, man and dog crawled at a fast clip. When Leo reached her side, he positioned her behind him then motioned to one of the officers to join them.

When the lawman made it to their side, Leo told him, "I need you to keep her safe. I'm going after the creep." He grabbed the leash dangling from True's collar and veered to the left to disappear into the woods.

Alicia's heart slammed against her breastbone. She wanted to yank Leo back to her side, to keep him from pursuing the lunatic bent on killing her. Fear tightened a noose around her neck. What if Leo ended up hurt? Or worse?

Leo led True in a semicircle so that they'd end up behind the shooter. He caught a glimpse of a man through the branches. It was the killer Alicia had seen. Determined to end the guy's reign of terror over Alicia, Leo crept closer. Suddenly the man whipped around and aimed his weapon in their direction.

Grabbing True by the collar, Leo yanked him behind a fallen tree trunk just as the thug fired. The dull thud of the bullet hitting the log reverberated through Leo. He clenched his jaw, unwilling to return fire in case his bullet missed. He wouldn't risk hitting Alicia or any of the cops working the crime scene.

Taking a chance he could talk the guy down, Leo called out, "Put down your weapon. You've nowhere to go."

Leo heard a snort and then the sound of the guy running away as he crashed through the trees and underbrush away from where Alicia was hidden. Leo dropped his head back against the log. "Thank You, Lord, for Your protection." He needed to get back to Alicia.

After a heartbeat, he and True rapidly made their way back to the water's edge. "He escaped into the woods," he announced.

Alicia and the two uniformed officers came out from behind the cottonwood tree and went in search of the gunman's trail. The forensic team emerged from their hiding places.

Leo spoke to the forensic lead investigator. "Can we take the boat back to the marina? I need to get Ms. Duncan out of here. I'll send back more officers."

"That's fine," the gray-haired tech said. "We'll be here awhile. Just return the boat as soon as possible."

"Will do." Leo hurried to Alicia. "We're getting out of here."

She held the puppy to her chest. The poor dog's body was racked with tremors. "The puppy belonged to Sue Ellen."

His heart squeezed tight. "We'll see if her family will take him."

She nodded and set River on the ground. True came over to sniff the younger Lab. "And if not?"

He helped her into the boat, careful to keep his body a barrier between her line of sight and the body in the water. "Would you want to adopt him?"

"I'm not sure I'm ready for a young dog," she said as she took a seat. River lay down at her feet next to True. "I'm just now getting used to the idea of having dogs around."

Leo started the boat engine. Soon they were zipping

along the water toward the marina. Leo sat so that Alicia was blocked from view by anyone on shore.

He appreciated her honesty. Caring for a canine took time and commitment. It wasn't something anyone should venture into lightly. "I could take him to Billings to be trained as an officer in honor of Jake," he said as guilt once again pinched him.

She laid a hand on his arm. "What happened to Jake?"

"I failed him," he admitted. "I was supposed to have his back."

"Julianne said you could have been the one abducted instead."

"I wish it had been me," he stated flatly.

"Don't say that," she chided. "If you'd been the one taken, you wouldn't be here to protect me."

"No, Jake would. He's a better man than me."

"I don't know this Jake person, obviously. But you're a good man, Agent Leo Gallagher. Don't doubt that."

"You don't know me," he said hoarsely. "You don't know what I've done."

"Certainly nothing worth condemning yourself for."

He stared into her pale, beautiful, trusting eyes. "I let my little sister die."

TEN

I let my little sister die.

Leo's words bounced through Alicia's head. She'd had to strain to hear him over the roar of the powerboat's engine and the sound of the wind rushing past as they raced toward the marina. She couldn't have heard him right.

He'd let his little sister die? What happened? When? How? The questions formed but all she could do was stare into his bleak green eyes. It seemed her voice had deserted her. Out of shock or dread?

They docked and debarked to an awaiting police escort. She coaxed the puppy out of the boat and then onto the floor of the front passenger seat of Leo's SUV, and then she slid in herself, the whole while aching with the need to…what?

She wasn't sure. Comfort Leo?

She tightened her hold on the leash secured to River's collar. She didn't know the story. Maybe he wasn't the good guy she'd believed him to be. Yet she had a hard time reconciling that thought with the kind, honorable man she was coming to know.

But then again, she'd learned the hard way people could easily hide their true selves.

After Leo secured True in his special compartment, he jumped in the driver's seat and drove them back to the ranch. The puppy curled at her feet and fell asleep. She watched the town of Settler's Valley pass by. There'd been a time when she'd been so eager to leave this town and the valley, but now she couldn't imagine a prettier place to live.

They hit the two-lane highway leading east through flat pastureland that stretched for miles and eventually ran into the Blackthorn Mountains. She turned her gaze to the man sitting behind the wheel of the black SUV. Did she dare ask him about his sister? Did she want to know?

The debate within herself raged on, keeping her from speaking. On the one hand, she wanted to get to the truth. Was he really responsible for his sister's death or were his words overly dramatic? What good would come from knowing what had happened in his past? Would it make her trust him less? Or more? Would knowing the burdens he carried make him more real, more accessible? Did she want him to be?

No. She wanted to keep him at a safe distance from her heart. If she were to ever risk falling in love again, it would have to be with someone who wouldn't put his career first. Someone who wouldn't put his own selfish desires ahead of her and Charlie.

Though Leo hadn't shown any signs of selfishness, he was a dedicated lawman. She couldn't compete with the job again. She'd had enough of that with Jeff.

When they reached the ranch, she hopped out before Leo even turned off the engine. She gathered the puppy in her arms. River licked her face and she grimaced as she realized she'd made a huge mistake bringing the dog into their lives. Charlie was going to go nuts for him.

And if she wasn't careful, she'd lose her heart to the puppy as well. Leo released True before coming around to where she stood on the other side of the vehicle.

"Everything okay?" he asked.

His shuttered expression made her wince inwardly. He probably thought she was judging him, condemning him the way he seemed to be condemning himself. "Yes. I was just thinking that bringing home this pup might confuse Charlie."

Leo's eyes softened. "We'll have to be clear that he's a guest and will be leaving. Like me."

Her heart dropped a beat at the reminder. Confusion swirled around her like a tornado. Hadn't she just told herself she wanted distance from him? It was dumb for her to feel dejected. Wasn't it? "Right. Leaving."

"Let me take him." Leo held out his arms.

As sweet and cute as she found the puppy, she knew giving him to Leo was for the best. She didn't want to let herself become too attached to the dog or to the man standing beside her. She released the puppy into Leo's waiting arms. He held the squirming dog with firm but gentle hands. For a moment she imagined him holding a newborn child and her heart sighed with longing. Having grown up alone, without siblings or even cousins, she'd always hoped to have a large family.

Resigned to never having that dream fulfilled, she yanked her gaze away from Leo and River and walked determinedly to the house. Charlie was her world. That was all she needed.

As soon as she entered the house, Charlie jumped from her dad's lap and raced toward her. He flung his arms around her knees, nearly knocking her backward. "Whoa, little man."

His round face beamed up at her. "Mommy!"

She knelt down and hugged her son tight, as love for him overwhelmed her. "I missed you today."

"Puppy?" Charlie wiggled out of her arms to stare up at the yellow Lab in Leo's arms.

She let out a wry laugh. How could she compete with a dog?

Leo squatted down so that Charlie and the pup were on the same level. "This is River. He's going to be a guest. Is that okay, kiddo?"

Charlie's nose scrunched up in confusion. Alicia ruffled his hair. "River is staying with us for a few days, just like Leo and True."

"Do you want to pet him?" Leo asked Charlie.

Charlie nodded and put out a hand.

"Let him sniff you first," Leo instructed.

River smelled Charlie's hand then licked his knuckles. Charlie's giggle lifted Alicia's spirits. Her son had an infectious laugh.

True came to join the lovefest and also licked Charlie on the face, eliciting more peals of laughter. Charlie snuggled into the crook of Leo's arm and hitched himself up on Leo's bent knee. Over Charlie's head, Alicia met Leo's tender gaze and her insides turned to mush. The man clearly had a soft spot for her son.

Both overjoyed and saddened by the affection building between Charlie and Leo, she offered him a smile. One corner of his mouth lifted in an engaging half grin that stole her breath. A ribbon of yearning wound through her, making her wish that same affection had been directed at her.

Ridiculous, of course. But she was helpless to stem the rising desire for affection, connection and…did she dare think it? Love.

She really needed to get a grip and control her reactions to this man. It wasn't good for her or Charlie to let themselves become emotionally involved.

"What do we have here?" Dad asked, drawing Alicia's focus away from Leo.

"We found this little guy in the woods," she replied. She drew her father away so that she could explain fully without Charlie hearing.

Dad shook his head as anger and sadness flashed in his eyes. "What is this world coming to?"

"It's shocking to have something this horrible happen— *twice*—so close to home." She felt bad that she'd brought danger to his doorstep by being in the wrong place at the wrong time.

Yet if she hadn't seen the killer, then the police wouldn't know whom to search for. God had put her where He needed her. She had to trust that He had a plan and He would protect them.

She didn't know how people suffered tragedy or horror without faith. She continually clung to the knowledge that God existed and that He loved her. Without that, life seemed so bleak.

"Alicia, do you have another water bowl for River?" Leo asked.

"Of course." In the kitchen she found a small bowl identical to the one she'd given him to use for True.

After filling it with cold tap water, she set it down. River immediately squirmed to be set free from Leo's hold. He let go of the dog and River lapped greedily at the water. Charlie sat on the floor nearby, waiting patiently to play again with the young dog. True drank from his bowl then moved to lie down in front of the front door.

"I need to go check on the horses and feed them," she said, glancing at the clock. She hadn't fed them before heading to town this morning. And though she knew they'd have plenty of grass to forage on in the pasture, she wanted to supplement with some hay and grain.

"I'll take care of them," Leo said firmly. "You stay here with your family. Rest. You've had enough stress for today."

Choosing to take his words as an offer rather than a directive, she said, "I appreciate that you want to help, but there's so much to be done. Besides feeding them, you'll need to check their hooves and put sunscreen on their noses."

"Sunscreen?"

"Didn't you notice Apple's cute pink nose?" She watched as understanding dawned on his handsome face.

"I'll bet she does need sunscreen. Can do," he assured her. "And the hooves will be no problem. I've worked with horses before, remember?"

"So you said." Deciding it would be easier to let him care for the horses than to argue with him, she nodded. "Fine. But if you run into trouble, I'll come help. Meanwhile, I'll do the watering."

"I can do that while I'm outside."

She frowned, not liking the idea of being a prisoner inside her own home. "We should have stopped at the grocery store on the way back from town." Of course, having just been shot at had pushed everything else from her mind.

"Make a list," Leo said. "I'll call the grocery store with the order and have them deliver it."

She fought back a chuckle. "They don't deliver. That's a city thing."

"Then I'll call Chief Jarrett and ask him to have an officer go pick up the order and bring it out here."

"You have a solution for everything, don't you, Agent Gallagher?" The man liked to problem-solve.

He grinned. "I try. What else can I help you with?"

She watched Charlie and River playing with a dish-rag Dad had given them.

"The vacuuming, the dusting, the toilets." She rattled off all the household chores that were waiting for atten-tion. He'd no doubt leave those to her. In her experience, men tended to leave that sort of work to the women. Even in these modern times of nannies and stay-at-home dads. The moms of her students would commiserate with each other that men just didn't clean the house.

When she'd returned to her childhood home, she'd found Dad had done very little, if any, cleaning after Mom died. The place had been a mess. Of course, he'd been still grieving and alone, so he hadn't felt the need to clean.

Once she and Charlie moved in, though, Dad had stepped up. At least in the kitchen. He kept the dishes washed and the counters spotless. Her late husband, on the other hand, had outright laughed when she'd asked for help with the housekeeping.

"That's women's work," he'd said. She hadn't real-ized until after their honeymoon that he'd expected her to be the one to take care of their home while he worked. Even though she was going to school full-time and later took a job teaching. They had a small place, so it hadn't been much work, and she liked a neat and tidy place.

Leo didn't even blink. "When I'm done with the horses, I'll take care of the housework."

She dropped her chin. "Really?"

"Yes, really."

She shook her head. "You don't have to. I was joking."

He shrugged. "It's no big deal. I can clean with the best."

"I'll keep that in mind," she said. "Thankfully last night's fire didn't take all of the hay and grains. If you put a bale and two scoops of grains in a bucket inside the gate then whistle, the horses should come. There's enough grass in the pasture for them to forage on, but I'd still like to give them some food." She moved to the cabinet, where she kept Charlie's sunscreen. "Here. Just rub a dab of this onto their noses."

He took the tube of lotion, their fingers brushing. The slight contact shouldn't have been a big deal but a tingle raced up her arm, reminding her of how good it had felt earlier to hold his hand. She wondered what it would be like to kiss him. Her gaze was drawn to his mouth and yearning pulled at her.

Uh-oh. Not something she should be thinking about. She didn't need kisses. And she doubted very much that Leo would be inclined to give them to her.

She jerked back. His eyebrow hitched up a notch. To cover her embarrassing reaction, she tucked her hands behind her back and said, "Do you have the house phone number? If you get into trouble or need help, you should call."

He took out his cell phone. "Give it to me, Alicia."

After giving him the number, she grabbed a bag of baby carrots from the refrigerator and walked him to the door. "They love these," she said and offered him the bag.

"Thanks." He took the bag and stuffed it into one of the pockets of his pants. "I'll let the officers outside know to be extra alert while I'm gone."

She knew he was doing this to keep her out of the line of sight should the shooter decide to try another attempt at silencing her. She laid a hand on his arm. The muscle beneath her palm jumped. "Thank you, Leo," she said. "I appreciate all you're doing to keep me and my family safe."

He briefly covered her hand with his. "I— It's my job." He and True walked out the door.

"That young man is a good guy," Dad pronounced.

She spun from the door to stare. She'd never heard her father give anyone but her mother and Charlie a compliment. "You like him."

"That I do." He pinned her with an intense stare. "So do you."

Her face flamed. "Yes. He's a well-trained agent here to protect me. What's not to like?"

"Nothing. Too bad you hadn't met him instead of that—"

"Dad!" She cut him off before he could say something derogatory about Jeff in front of Charlie. She glanced over to where Charlie sat with River. The dog had fallen asleep to Charlie's rhythmic petting.

Dad's lips twisted, like he'd tasted something sour. "All I'm saying is Agent Gallagher's a keeper, as your mother says."

Her heart pinched at her dad's use of present tense

when referring to her mother. But he was right. Mom would have liked him, too. "I hardly know the man. We have a strictly professional relationship."

Dad snorted and went back to his recliner. "Yeah, sweetheart, you keep telling yourself that."

Was her attraction to the handsome federal agent that transparent? She hoped that Leo wasn't aware of her feelings. Alicia put a hand to her stomach to quell the sudden queasy sensation rocketing through her. What was she doing?

"There you go, Apple." Leo applied a dollop of sun-screen to the soft pink tip of the reddish-brown quarter horse's nose. Though the sun was beginning to set now, the sun protection would last for a few days at least.

The horse blew air through its teeth and trotted away. The other two horses had already had their hooves cleaned and their sun protection slathered on before wandering off. Leo stroked Apple's neck and offered her a carrot from the bag Alicia had given him.

He smiled whenever she came to mind. The response was involuntary, just like his attraction to the pretty widow. He had to get a grip. Stay focused.

True let out a bark, drawing Leo's attention. The dog was pacing along the fence, sniffing the ground. His ears were back and his tail high. He'd caught a whiff of something he found threatening. Leo hurried over.

There were shoe impressions in the dirt on the other side of the fence as if someone had stopped there to take in the scenery. Leo turned around. From here there was a clear view to the house, about six hundred feet away.

Irritation mixed with agitation slithered along his nerves. Had their unidentified suspect been bold enough to come this close to the house? When? Had this been where he'd stood when he'd blown up the barn? Or had he watched them leave this morning and followed them to the river? Was that how he'd found them? He took out his cell phone and took pictures of the prints.

Tires crunching on the gravel drive alerted him to an approaching black SUV. He double-checked the pasture gate was locked and then hurried to meet the vehicle that was identical to the one he drove. Max and Julianne were back from Burns Junction.

He sent up a quick prayer they had news on Jake. And on the man targeting Alicia. When he'd called to update them on finding the second body in the river earlier, they'd had little to report and were angered by his news.

As he'd watched his boss and coworker drive away this morning, he'd been conflicted between his need to rescue Jake and his desire to protect Alicia. Only knowing that Max would turn over every rock and look under every tree had allowed Leo to stick to the commitment he'd made to guard Alicia. That and her trust and confidence in him.

He couldn't believe he'd confessed his deepest, darkest secret to her. Few people knew his story.

What was even more unbelievable was she hadn't peppered him with questions, hadn't demanded to know the details or recoiled from him in disgust as he feared she would once she learned the truth. He could only hope she wasn't curious enough about the revelation to eventually ask for more specifics.

And if she wasn't curious, then that could only mean she had no feelings for him beyond the need of safety. The thought left him depressed. Which didn't make sense. His job was to keep her safe, not to want her to fall for him and vice versa.

He stopped in his tracks. Fall for her? Hardly.

The anxiousness in his gut begged to differ.

"Hey," Max called as he stepped from his vehicle. He wore sunglasses that hid his gaze, but the disfiguring scar on his face was still visible.

Leo lifted a hand in greeting and jogged the rest of the way. "Any news on Jake?"

Julianne came around the front end. Her dark hair hung down her back in a ponytail caught at her nape with a band that blended in with the color of her hair. "Unfortunately, no. We showed his picture and Angus Dupree's to every person we came across in Burns Junction, Drytown and at every rest stop and gas station in between."

Leo's heart sank that his prayer would go unanswered for now.

"There were, however, several sightings of the mysterious killer," Max added. "He was seen hanging around town the day Virginia Carter disappeared. As far as we can tell, she went for a hike in the forest and never returned to her hotel."

Leo's hand clenched. "He followed her and then brutally murdered her."

"That's my take on it," Max agreed. "The local authorities are combing the woods looking for the primary crime scene. They'll contact me when they find it."

"We gave a copy of the killer's image to the Drytown police as well as an image of Jake and Dupree," Julianne said. "They will distribute the photos to their officers, who will ask around town. No one at Sue Ellen Bishop's hair salon recognized any of the men in the pictures. Last anyone saw her, she was heading home from the salon. She was single, lived alone and had no family to speak of."

Seeing the sadness on Julianne's face, Leo put his hand on her shoulder. "I'm sure her clients will miss her."

She nodded. They all hurt when they were unable to save the innocent from harm.

"We'll head back that way in the morning to search for Jake," Max said. "Though I suspect if Dupree had Jake stashed away in Wyoming, it would be off the beaten path. Dupree wouldn't risk easy exposure."

The front door to the house opened and Alicia stepped out. She'd twisted her long dark hair into a knot on the top of her head and stray tendrils curled around her face. The sleeves of her shirt were rolled up and an apron covered her jeans. Leo's heart lurched in his chest at the sight of her.

"You're just in time for dinner," she called to them. "Come, wash up."

"A homemade meal," Max said, patting his stomach. "That's a bonus."

Leo grimaced as he remembered his promise to have her grocery list delivered. He'd spent too much time walking the ranch, watering and dealing with the horses. There was nothing he hated more than when he didn't live up to his word. He hustled to the house intent on apologizing, then suddenly stopped himself.

That was what someone in a relationship would do. He was here to protect her and her family. Nothing more.

He had to get his head right or it would cost someone he cared about. Again.

ELEVEN

That night after dinner, Alicia couldn't believe how content she was. The house was full of people and dogs. Julianne and Charlie were playing I Spy on the floor surrounded by four canines, each happily chewing on a bone.

Dad and Max had disappeared into her father's den. She wasn't sure what the two would find to converse about; her dad wasn't normally the most talkative person.

It had been surprising and fascinating how congenial he'd been during the meal, regaling the agents with stories of his childhood on his family's farm in Idaho.

Stories Alicia had never heard.

He'd told them about falling in love with Mom the moment he'd set eyes on her during a trip to Wyoming with his brother, who was looking to buy a horse in Settler's Valley.

Though Alicia had heard that particular story from Mom over the years, she'd never heard her father's rendition. There had been a part of Alicia that had thought Mom was romanticizing her and Dad's romance, but her father's version was even more romantic.

She'd spent the meal squashing the urge to look in Leo's direction. She told herself she only wanted to gauge his reaction to her father's story of true love, but she knew in her heart her wish to lock eyes with him stemmed from a more dangerous place. A place she refused to shine a light on at the moment. Maybe ever.

As Alicia scrubbed the pot she'd made the spaghetti sauce in, she continued to find herself yearning for a second chance at love. Not the stars-in-the-eyes relationship she'd had with Jeff. She'd been so blinded by the need to be loved, she hadn't seen the signs that he wasn't the man she'd hoped he'd be.

No, Alicia wanted a relationship built on mutual trust and respect. She wanted to fall in love with someone who would put family first. Maybe that was unrealistic. Maybe she'd never find anyone like that.

But it wouldn't hurt to ask God to bring someone special into her life for her and Charlie to love and be loved by.

"Where are the dish towels?" Leo asked as he brought in the last of the dishes from the table. "I'll dry."

Surprise washed over her. "Really? You want to help with the dishes?"

"Of course. Why wouldn't I help? You made the dinner. It's only right I should clean up. In fact, if you'd like to go be with Charlie, I can take over."

"Wow, that's…very thoughtful of you." She glanced to where Charlie leaned against Julianne while they played their game. "I think Charlie is well occupied. Besides, I'm already elbow-deep into scrubbing."

He let out a deep, masculine chuckle. "So, dish towel?"

Since her hands were soapy and wet, she pointed

with the toe of her tennis shoe to the second-to-bottom drawer on her right. "Thank you."

"It's the least I can do for that wonderful meal after flaking on getting your groceries." He bent and grabbed the top towel.

She shook her head. "Stop. You've already apologized, though there was no need. We have enough supplies for another couple of days. It's not urgent."

"I will reimburse you for all the food we've eaten," he said as he grabbed the fry pan from the drying rack and towel-dried it.

She faced him. "That is not necessary. Dad and I are happy to provide for you and the other agents. You're here protecting us. There's no way we could ever repay you other than to be hospitable."

He smiled and inclined his head. "All right, I'll accept your generosity without conditions. Thank you."

She returned his smile. "You're welcome."

"I take it your late husband wasn't one for helping in the kitchen," Leo said, his voice soft.

Checking to see that Charlie wasn't paying attention to them, she lowered her voice to answer, "No. Jeff was, as he'd like to say, old-fashioned. The wife cooked and cleaned. The husband took care of the yard and house repairs." She sniffed. "Personally, I think his mom did too much for him and he never learned to care for himself. I was too naive to realize what I was getting myself in for when I married him."

"You weren't happy in your marriage?"

After another peek at Charlie, she murmured, "No. Not for a long time."

She pulled the garbage can from beneath the sink and removed the liner, tying the top into a knot.

"Here, let me take that." Leo reached for the bag.

Relinquishing her hold, she said, "I'll show you where it goes."

She led him to the back door and out to the side yard. He tossed the trash bag in the large can. She moved a few feet away to stare at the charred remains of the barn. Leo stepped behind her and tugged her into the shadows.

To protect her. The thought warmed her from the inside out.

He was so close she could feel the heat of his body, could smell the spicy aftershave clinging to his skin. She wanted to lean into him and have him wrap his arms around her and tell her all would be well.

"I'm sorry you were unhappy," he murmured.

"Not your fault." And it wasn't.

She realized she shouldn't hold Jeff's transgressions against all men. It'd been six months since his death and in that time she'd kept every interested male at bay because she'd decided she couldn't trust a man to keep his promises or his commitments.

Yet here stood a man whom she could trust, a man of integrity who honored his word and lived up to every dream she ever had of what a man should be. A scary temptation to let her guard down. To give in to not only the attraction arcing between them, but also to the affection and care burrowing deep into her heart.

"What happened between you two?" he asked curiously.

"Age-old story—I wasn't enough to keep his interest and he wasn't willing to be monogamous."

Leo's hands cupped her shoulders, his breath warm on her neck. She didn't feel trapped as she would have had it been anyone else. Instead, the heat of his palms penetrated the thin cotton of her T-shirt and made her heart race.

"I'm sorry he wasn't true to you," Leo rasped close to her ear. "He was an idiot. Not all men are that way."

She swallowed before she could speak. "I'm still struggling to learn that. I had hoped once Charlie was born Jeff would change, but he never wanted children. He never bonded with Charlie. In fact, having a baby drove Jeff further away."

The disgusted growl that came from Leo was gratifying in a strange way. "He didn't deserve you or Charlie. Children are a gift from God to be cherished."

"And wives?" she asked before she could think better of it.

He released her. "And definitely wives."

She turned to face him. It was too dark to see his expression but the sudden tension emanating from him was unmistakable. She had so many questions she wanted to ask. Like why wasn't he married? Did he ever want to settle down? Raise a family?

Questions that would only lead her into dangerous territory because she was afraid of the answers and what they would mean to her heart.

Instead, she gathered her courage and went back to the dramatic bombshell he'd dropped earlier that day. "What happened with your little sister?"

Leo sucked in a sharp breath, even though he'd suspected they'd come to this. He'd have to face the choice to give her the details of his horrible secret or walk away, effectively damaging whatever fledgling relationship they were building. Which he should do, if he was smart. Walking away would be easier and safer for them both. But he'd never be able to keep her protected if she didn't trust him.

She reached out to place a hand over his heart. "You can trust me with your story."

He nearly snorted as she echoed his thoughts. Trusting her wasn't the problem.

"I want to know you, Leo. I won't judge you."

He gave her a wry smile, though he knew she couldn't see it. He judged himself enough for them both. He wasn't sure where to start. The beginning seemed the best option.

"My parents were messed up. There's no other way to say it. Dad was an abusive alcoholic. Mom was—" Compassion for the woman who'd given birth to him spread through his chest. "She'd just turned eighteen when she got pregnant with me. My father was twenty."

"So young."

The compassion in her voice wrapped around him. "They ran away together and tried to make things work."

"How old were you when your sister came along?"

"I was five. She was the most beautiful thing to happen to me. I loved her so much." He blinked to keep the burn of tears back. "My parents left me to care for her while they worked or were at the bar."

"They left a five-year-old to care for an infant?"

The outrage in her voice touched him deeply. "Crazy, huh? I took care of her instead of going to school. We'd move anytime someone reported that I wasn't enrolled at the local elementary school."

"That must have been so frightening for you and your sister."

"I was Jen's world. She came to me when she was hurt or tired or hungry."

"That's a great deal of responsibility to put on a child."

He bit the inside of his cheek, welcoming the pain to counteract the sorrow and torment in his heart. "When she was a little over two I was watching her one afternoon and I really needed to use the restroom. I put her in her playpen. But she'd grown so tall and was a little monkey. It never dawned on me she'd climb out. But she did."

Alicia's arms slid around his waist as if she sensed the horror about to come.

He couldn't stop himself from placing his arms around her. She felt so good in his embrace and gave him the courage to relive that horrible day. "When I came out of the bathroom, she was gone. She'd managed to get the sliding glass door open and squeezed through the broken slats of the back gate. I went after her but I was too late. She'd wandered into the street and was struck by a car. She died instantly."

"Oh, Leo," Alicia breathed, her voice choked with emotion. "I'm so sorry. You never should have been put in that position. You were just a child yourself."

"That's what the judge said," he told her. "My parents both served time for negligent homicide. I was taken into child protective custody and sent to live in a series of foster homes until I ran away at fourteen."

"Where did you go?"

"Andale, Kansas. I earned enough money mowing lawns for the neighbors of the last foster parents but Andale was as far as the money would get me on the bus."

Moisture glimmered in her eyes. "How did you survive?"

"I lived on the street. People in Andale were kind,

though. And there were shelters. I bluffed my way to a job on a horse ranch. The old-geezer foreman, Ben Smith, took me under his wing." Affection for the man who'd changed his life lifted his spirit. "Ben insisted if I was going to work and live on the ranch that I had to enroll in high school. I don't know how he knew I was only fourteen but he did. He took me to the admissions office and signed me up, stating he was my guardian."

"He sounds like a wonderful man."

"He was. He pushed me to do well in school and helped me get into college on scholarships and work-study. I miss him. He passed on from lung cancer right after I graduated from university."

"I'm sure he was proud of you," she said softly. "I'm proud of you."

Her words made his eyes burn with unshed tears. "Thank you, Alicia. That means a lot to me. Though I'm not sure I deserve it. I've been letting a lot of people down lately."

She tightened her hold and laid her cheek on his shoulder. He kissed her forehead, breathing in the floral scent of her shampoo.

She tilted her head up and pressed her lips against his. Sensations exploded through him, sending sparks through his veins, along his nerve endings. He deepened the kiss, reveling in the feel of her, the taste of her. She felt so good, so right, in his arms. Like they were meant for each other.

His mind clanged with warning bells that this was too much. He should release her and step away before they both got burned by the emotional fallout of giving in to their attraction.

But the way he'd been singed by the barn fire was

nothing compared to the effect she had on him. He knew deep down the scars she'd leave on his soul would be far more permanent than what he'd suffered after saving the horses from the inferno caused by the drone explosion. Yet his heart refused to let him release her.

He wanted this. Had wanted to kiss her from the moment she'd walked into the chief's office. There'd been such apprehension and courage shining from her pale blue eyes that drew him in. He'd been immediately attracted but it had been at the river when he'd felt the shift in his heart. She'd stood on the boulder, so pretty and fierce, bravely taking a stand for the unknown victim in the river.

He could tell himself that whatever this was that was happening between them was a mistake all he wanted. But he knew what that shift meant, even though the thought terrified him. He'd been struck with something he hadn't really believed existed. Love. Or at least the beginnings of love.

Old man Howard's story of falling instantly in love with his wife had resonated with Leo. He'd been confused by it, but now...

He'd never bought into the whole love-at-first-sight thing. That was too fantastical to be believed. Had he heard Harmon's account of meeting his wife a week ago, Leo would have scoffed. But not now.

As crazy as it sounded, he had to admit he was falling for Alicia.

And that was reason enough to give him the strength to break the kiss and step back.

He couldn't do this to her.

Refused to lead her on. He wasn't the marrying kind. His job came first, and his guilt and remorse for the past would always haunt him. He couldn't be responsible for the happiness of anyone else.

"We should go in." His voice betrayed him with its huskiness.

"O-okay."

The confusion in her tone made him flinch. But it was for the best. He guided her inside.

Max and Julianne were at the dining table with the computer and were live-streaming with Dylan.

"Your dad took Charlie for a bath," Julianne said to Alicia.

"Great. Thanks," she replied, her voice sounding overly bright to him. He suppressed a wince.

"Hey, Dylan has an ID on the killer," Max informed him.

Pushing aside his own personal torment, Leo kicked into gear and strode forward with Alicia matching his stride. "What do you have?" he asked Dylan.

"The facial recognition turned up too many potential matches. So after learning that the unidentified subject had been seen at the hotel where Virginia Carter stayed, I hacked into the hotel's video feed, with their permission, of course." He flashed a wry grin. "Anyway, the perp is careful to avert his face from the camera, but I captured his body movements and the overall structure of his physique to run through another software program that compared all factors to find a ninety-three percent match."

Leo reined in his impatience and calmly said, "Bottom line, Dylan?"

"Oh, right. Sorry. You probably don't care how I obtained the information," the techie said. "Bottom line, the unidentified suspect is Garry Pike from Ventura, California."

An image with stats appeared on the screen of a Caucasian male, five-five, dark brown eyes, brown hair and thick facial hair.

"He's got a rap sheet a mile long," Dylan continued. "In the photos I can find of him, he's got long hair and a beard. And his nose has either been broken in the last few years or he's had a horrible nose job."

"He's got the same dead eyes," Alicia commented.

"Good work, buddy," Max said. "I knew you wouldn't let us down."

Dylan looked pleased by the compliment. "Thanks, boss. I hope you find the creep."

"Can you get this information to Christy? I want his name and image on the news, pronto," Max said.

"Will do."

"Hey, Dylan, how's Zara faring?" Julianne asked conversationally.

Worry crossed the younger man's face. "Not sure. She mentioned some trouble affecting her group of trainees. She couldn't go into details, but she's concerned the group might not graduate on time."

"How will that affect the wedding?" Julianne queried.

Dylan rubbed his jaw. "We'll have to postpone if she doesn't make it home in time."

Leo's heart went out to the guy. Dylan was obviously upset by the prospect of putting off his wedding. Dylan and Zara had gone through their own ordeal not that long ago, before Zara went off to the FBI training academy.

Thinking of weddings and marriage, Leo's gaze met Alicia's. He immediately yanked his focus away. Man, he had to stop this. He knew it would be the most difficult assignment of his life. She was like a magnet to him. Pulling him closer without effort and it would take everything in him to resist.

Something beeped on Dylan's end, drawing Leo's attention away from the mesmerizing woman who consumed his thoughts.

"Whoa," the young man said. "An alert just came through from the sheriff's department in a town called Basin. One of the deputies spotted Jake."

Leo jolted as if hit by a bolt of lightning. Through the ringing in his ears, he heard Max say, "Text me the name and the address of the department. Julianne and I will head there now."

"On it. Talk to you later." Dylan disappeared from the screen and Julianne shut down the computer.

Anticipation raced through Leo. They were so close to rescuing Jake from the clutches of Angus Dupree. Leo wanted to go with his boss. He wanted to be the one to find Jake. To bring him home safely since Leo had been the one to fail at watching his fellow agent's back. A soft hand on his arm startled him.

"Go with them," Alicia said. "We'll be safe here while you're gone."

Suddenly the ringing in his ears ceased. There was no question in his mind that he wasn't leaving her. Not even to appease his guilt. He shook his head and covered her hand. "I promised you I'd protect you. I don't break my promises."

The relief on her pretty face was worth staying for. To Max, Leo said, "Keep me informed."

"Of course." His boss whistled and Opal, who'd been sleeping under the front window, jumped to her feet. The other three K-9s also came alert, aware that it was time to go to work.

True came to sit beside Leo, and Thunder went to Julianne. The puppy, River, watched from his spot in front of the fireplace. He rose to his feet as if sensing something was happening and he wanted to be a part of it. One day he would, Leo thought fondly. After he was trained, he'd be a good K-9 officer.

"I'll let you know if we're going to make it back tonight or not," Julianne told him before she and Thunder disappeared out the front door.

Max nodded and then exited, closing the door behind him.

True whined, clearly wanting to join in the work. Leo touched the chocolate Lab's head. "We're needed here, boy."

"Thank you," Alicia said. "I know what a sacrifice you're making."

Leo shook his head. "No sacrifice. This is where I'm supposed to be. You're the priority."

Her beautiful blue eyes misted and her top teeth tugged on her bottom lip, reminding him of their unforgettable kiss. His mouth went dry. He wanted to pull her to him and kiss her again. His fingers curled in an effort to refrain from reaching for her.

"I'm going to walk the perimeter and check on the horses," he said as he backed toward the door. To True, he said, "Stay here. Guard Alicia."

The confusion and the hint of hurt in her eyes chased him out the door as he escaped as quickly as he could. He headed straight for the pasture gate and whistled. Three dark shapes materialized from the gloom. He dug out the bag of carrots he still had in his pants pocket and offered one to each horse.

"What am I going to do?" he asked out loud. How

was he going to leave Alicia and Charlie behind when it came time to go?

They'd wiggled under his skin, found the hole in his heart and had quickly filled it.

He hoped he could walk away when the time came. Because he really had no other choice.

The horses still had hay, so Leo walked around the charred barn and the two other outbuildings that housed the big equipment needed to run a ranch. A mower, a front-end loader, an ATV and a snowplow.

Though his gaze was alert, his mind kept turning over all the possibilities of how he and Alicia could have a shot at anything together and continually came up empty. Even if he was willing to risk his heart, to risk letting someone close and risk failing them, how could he leave his job? How could she leave the ranch?

He was being ridiculous even contemplating a romance with the pretty widow. He wasn't sure how deep her feelings went. And knew he shouldn't trust her feelings. She'd been through several traumatic events the past couple of days. He was an easy target for emotions that were running too high.

As he passed the Chevy truck, the slight scrape of metal against metal was the only warning he had before a stunning blow connected with the back of his skull. Grunting, he went down to his knees. He twisted toward his attacker, blindly reaching out to grab his assailant. His nails dug into muscled flesh. A looming shadow brought down a large object to crash into Leo's temple.

The last thought he had before the world went dark was that he'd failed Alicia. He'd failed the woman he loved.

TWELVE

Alicia curled her feet beneath her on the couch as she waited for Leo to return from his patrol outside the ranch house. She'd changed from her earlier outfit into jeans and a flowered top. Charlie was upstairs asleep and Dad had retired for the night a little while ago, leaving her alone with her thoughts. Her mind was abuzz with the revelations she'd learned tonight. There was so much to take in and process.

Leo had had a rough and tragic childhood. He carried an undue burden from his neglectful parents. No child as young as he'd been should have been made responsible for the care of an infant or toddler. Why had God allowed such tragedy?

Alicia sighed. She knew blaming the Lord wasn't warranted. God gave humans free will.

The fact was, Leo's parents chose to put him in such a horrible position. They chose to mistreat their children and their carelessness cost a child her life, and Leo was still paying the price for that decision all these years later.

Alicia's heart ached with sorrow for a life cut short, her veins pulsing with anger at Leo's parents and her eyes burning with grief for Leo.

And to top off his burdens, Leo held himself responsible for his fellow agent's abduction. How messed up was that?

He didn't see that he couldn't have prevented Jake from being taken. Leo could have been the one kidnapped or, worse, killed trying to protect his friend.

Her insides twisted in knots at the thought of anything happening to Leo. She couldn't take it if he was injured while protecting her.

He was such a good man, a kind man. A man who didn't think he deserved happiness, because of his past.

The need to comfort and soothe away his pain gripped her tightly. But how could she console him? How could she ever alleviate a pain so deep?

She thought of her father and mother's love story. Dad walking into the mercantile, all swagger and bluster at nineteen. Mom had said it was the self-assurance that had caught her eye and drew her to him.

For Dad, Mom had been the prettiest girl he'd ever laid eyes on. She was working behind the counter in her father's store and had smiled at him. That was all it had taken, Dad had said.

Her mind jumped to that moment in the chief's office when Leo had turned around and she'd met his green-eyed gaze. And then he'd smiled. Something had altered in her heart, her life.

She gave herself a shake both physically and mentally.

Silly sentiment. Attraction, that was all.

Her father's voice echoed inside her head. *Yeah, you keep telling yourself that.*

True's low guttural growl sent a shudder of alarm over her. The dog stood staring at the front door. His silky brown ears were slanted forward and his pointy tail stood straight up and vibrated with the force of his agitation. Even River was disturbed.

The puppy had joined True in facing the front door. Only the puppy's ears were back and his tail tucked between his legs. He let out a high-pitched bark.

Adrenaline surging, Alicia jumped up from the couch. "What's wrong?"

Shaking her head at the silliness of asking the dogs a question neither could verbally answer, she moved to the window and peeked out through the curtain. The moon's glow shone on the Settler's Valley police car sitting dark in the driveway. She couldn't detect movement inside the car.

Dread filled her stomach and a knot of fear formed in her chest.

Where was Leo? He'd been gone a long time.

She grabbed the phone and called his cell. It rang then went to voice mail.

Her breathing grew shallow. Something was wrong. She dialed 911.

"Settler's Valley police station. What's your emergency?" the woman on the line calmly asked.

Feeling anything but calm, Alicia forced her voice to stay even. "This is Alicia Duncan. I'm not sure this is an emergency." She told herself she was panicking for no confirmed reason other than the horrible sensation that something wasn't right. And True's behavior supported her fears.

"There are two police officers sitting out in their car providing protection for my house," she said. "Would you mind contacting them and asking them to come knock on my door? I'm a bit spooked."

"One moment, please," the operator said and then clicked Alicia over to music while she held on.

A few seconds later the woman came back on. "Ma'am, are you safe?"

"Yes. I think so." Not liking the hint of intensity in the operator's tone, Alicia glanced up the staircase and vowed to protect Charlie at all costs. "What's happening?"

"We don't know, ma'am. The officers assigned to your protection are not responding. Chief Jarrett and more officers are on their way."

Her stomach sank. Alarm flooded her. "The FBI agent staying with us went outside and hasn't returned."

"I'll inform the chief," the woman said. "Please find a secure location inside the house and wait for officers to arrive."

True's growl turned into a deep bark filled with menace. He clawed at the door. He, no doubt, wanted to get to his partner. Or was the killer outside the door? She wasn't sure what to do. Did she let True leave? Or keep him close? Was Leo okay? Her heart caved in on the last thought. What if he was hurt and needed medical attention?

She ran to her dad's den and urgently tapped on the door. She heard Dad's shuffling feet, and then he yanked open the door.

"Why are you waking me up in the middle of the night?" he grumbled as he blinked at her with sleep in his eyes.

It was barely 10:00 p.m. but there was no point in arguing with him. "I need a gun." She pushed past him and hurried to the safe. Then tapped her foot in impatience.

Instantly, her dad's grogginess vanished. "What's happened? Where's Leo?"

"He went outside to walk the perimeter and hasn't returned. The dogs are going nuts. The officers in the patrol car are not responding. I have to find Leo and make sure he's—he's okay."

With a scowl of concern, Dad worked the lock on the safe and flung open the door. He grabbed his shotgun and then handed her a stainless-steel Walther .22 LR pistol. "Do you still know how to work this?"

"Of course, Dad." She palmed the weapon. He'd taught her how to use the handgun when she was young.

Since Wyoming was an open-carry state, he'd insisted she learn to shoot and that she take it with her when she rode alone, whether on the ranch or off, as a defense against predators. Though the mountain lions and coyotes that roamed Wyoming didn't normally attack unprovoked, it was wise to be prepared.

Dad put his robe on over his T-shirt and pajama bottoms, then slipped his bare feet into shoes. They hurried to the living room. True's agitation worsened. His barks grew more frantic. River whined. Alicia's tension increased tenfold. She sent up a silent plea that God would protect Leo.

Before opening the door, she said to her dad, "Keep Charlie safe."

"No. You stay here," he argued. "I'll go find Leo."

The man could hardly walk faster than a snail. There was no way she could let him go out there. But he was an accurate shot and could guard her son.

"I'm going. Your job is to keep my son safe." Carefully, she opened the front door and True shot out like a rocket, followed by River.

She moved to go after them when Dad grabbed her by the arm. "Caution. You don't know what's out there."

Taking a deep breath, she nodded and turned out the interior overhead light and the porch light. Moving into the shadows, she plastered her back against the exterior wall of the house and listened. Faintly in the distance she heard sirens.

The sound of True's growls and barks echoed all the way to the mountains. The dog was just to the right of the porch. Frightened, her knees weakened and her resolve to find Leo wavered. She should wait for the police.

But what if he was dying? He'd be angry with her for putting her life in danger. And she'd be no good to her son if she got herself killed.

Knowing the rational and smart thing to do was wait inside and pray, she shifted toward the door, intending to dart back into the house, but before she could slip through the doorway, a commotion broke out. True's snarls and barks filled the air.

A man's yelp, followed by a coarse curse, made her shiver. He was close. Too close for her comfort. And it wasn't Leo's voice.

She edged along the porch toward the uproar. A hulking man swung a stick, fending off True and River. Both dogs' jaws snapped as they attempted to bite the man.

With the weight of the .22 in her hands, Alicia ducked behind the railing and aimed toward the dark figure fighting with the dogs. She couldn't shoot at the man, not with the dogs moving in and out of her line of fire.

The police sirens were closer now. Just a few more moments, she thought desperately. If the dogs could keep the intruder from escaping, the police would be able to capture him and then normal life would resume.

There was a loud crack as the swinging stick struck True in the head, sending the dog flying and giving the intruder the opportunity to flee. River snapped at the man's feet and he kicked at him. The dog yelped and hopped back.

Alicia jumped up and yelled, "Stop or I'll shoot."

The assailant barely glanced back as he sprinted into the dark and disappeared from her view.

She ran down the porch stairs to where True had staggered to his feet. Glad to see the dog up and alive, she knelt beside him. "We need to find Leo," she told the dog. "Find Leo."

True lifted his nose to the air then whirled in the opposite direction and raced away. Alicia ran after him with River close at her heels. She'd lost sight of True. Then she heard his bark and followed the sound to the other side of Dad's old Chevy truck.

A dark form lay on the ground. True lay down next to him and whined. Leo. Anxiety twisted in her gut as she fell to her knees beside him. *Please, Lord, let him be alive.*

She couldn't stand the thought of losing him when she'd only just found him. She knew in her heart that she had fallen in love with this man. Her feelings defied logic. Defied her own sense of self-preservation even. Maybe it was a family thing that true love struck at first glance. Whatever the case, she wanted a chance to tell him. To find out what the future held for them.

Hoping against hope, she nudged his shoulder. "Leo. Leo, can you hear me?"

He didn't respond. Tears slipped down her cheeks. Would God deny her request?

With trembling fingers, she felt for a pulse at the side of his neck and her heart leaped when she found one. He wasn't dead. Joy burst through her and she slumped with relief. *Thank You, God.*

She attempted to move him but he weighed too much for her to budge him. She popped to her feet and ran toward the house, where Chief Jarrett and several other officers scrambled out of their cars. The headlights from the many vehicles shone on the house.

"Help!" she cried. "Agent Gallagher is hurt. Over this way!"

She ran back to Leo's side. The chief and another officer hustled over.

"Call for an ambulance," the chief instructed the officer. He put a hand on Alicia's shoulder. "Are you okay?"

"Yes, fine. The killer, the one I saw at the river, Garry Pike, was here. He hurt Leo and True. But he fled east, that way." She pointed in the direction the man had gone.

"I'll send officers to pursue," the chief said. "Hutchins, you stay here with Ms. Duncan and Agent Gallagher. Accompany the agent to the hospital."

The officer nodded. "Yes, sir."

"What happened to the two officers that were sitting outside the house?" she asked, half-afraid to hear the answer. Considering how many people Garry Pike had already killed, Alicia doubted two more would faze the criminal.

"Alive. The driver was Tasered and handcuffed to the steering wheel. The other was choked until he passed out. Seems the perp somehow got into the backseat and assaulted the officers."

Her dad, with Charlie in his arms, shuffled out of the house. Alicia couldn't let Charlie see Leo like this. Torn between wanting to stay with the unconscious agent and needing to protect her son, she felt ripped in two. But her son won out. "I'll be right back," she whispered to Leo, pressing a gentle kiss to his forehead, before she hurried to intercept her father and son. River raced alongside her while True kept watch over Leo.

Charlie reached out his arms for her. Swallowing back a sob, she took his familiar weight into her arms and held him snug against her chest. She breathed in his clean scent and closed her eyes, cherishing the moment, thankful for his safety.

"You okay, sweetheart?" her dad asked gruffly.

She met his gaze. "Yes."

"Agent Gallagher?"

"I don't know." The sting of tears had her blinking rapidly. "Can we take Charlie back inside?"

Her son leaned back to look into her face. "Police cars, Mommy."

"Yes, honey. We need to get out of their way," she told him. "They have a job to do."

She carried Charlie back into the house and got him a glass of water. And then settled River back on the blanket she'd laid out for him earlier.

Dad entered a moment later. Concern creased his brow. "An ambulance has arrived."

She nodded. "Can you stay with Charlie and River? I'm going with Leo."

"Of course. Call when you know anything. I'll answer." He took his grandson from her. "Come along, pal. Let's read a book."

Alicia watched them settle on the couch with a book.

River moved to lie at Dad's feet. Grabbing her purse, Alicia rushed outside in time to watch the paramedics lift the gurney carrying Leo's unconscious form into the back bay of the ambulance.

Before they could shut the doors, she jumped inside next to Officer Hutchins and on the floor lay True. The paramedic shrugged and shut the doors.

The ride to the nearest hospital took all of fifteen minutes. Leo remained unconscious the whole time. His handsome face was pale. Blood matted his hair. For such a big man, he seemed so vulnerable and exposed. Alicia held his hand and prayed.

Prayed that Leo would have no permanent damage from his injuries. That True would also not suffer any long-term effects from the blow to his head. She also prayed that Garry Pike would be found before anyone else was hurt.

Leo awoke with a splitting headache. He opened his eyes to the glare of overhead fluorescent lights and the annoying beeping of a machine hooked up to his chest. He immediately realized he was in a hospital. It took a full three seconds before memory rushed in.

He'd been attacked from behind. He'd been inattentive and distracted by his feelings for Alicia. And because of that he hadn't been alert enough to his attacker's presence. It was a move that could have cost him his life.

Alicia!

Oh, please, Lord, don't let my mistake have had dire consequences for her.

He ripped out the IV stuck to the back of his hand and yanked off the chest probes attached to the machine. The heart monitor signaled a loud alarm. Leo swung his feet over the side of the bed and stood. The room swayed. The door burst open, banging against the wall.

"What are you doing?" Alicia stormed into the room and grabbed him by the arm. A nurse and doctor were right on her heels.

His knees buckled as relief to see her unharmed flooded his system, washing away the spike of adrenaline that had prompted him up and out of the bed.

"You're okay?" he whispered in wonder.

"I am," she said and pushed him back onto the bed. "But you, mister, have a head wound and need to be lying down."

Happy to see her safe and sound, he complied. "And Charlie? Your dad?"

"Fine. Everyone is fine except you."

She moved back so the doctor and nurse could hook him back up to the monitors and IV, check his pupils and his vitals.

"Agent Gallagher," the doctor intoned.

He wore the prerequisite white lab coat with a stethoscope hanging around his neck. He appeared to be in his fifties with gray at his temples, a beak-like nose and sharp, intelligent eyes that made Leo think of a hawk. "You must rest. You suffered two nasty head contusions. One of which required sutures. We need to monitor you for a concussion."

He nodded and regretted the movement as a firestorm of pain swept through his brain.

Once the doctor and nurse left the room, Leo held out his hand for Alicia. She grasped it and curled her slender fingers around his.

"I'm sorry," he said. Regret and self-directed anger ate at his gut.

Her eyebrows pinched together in confusion. "Sorry? For what?"

"For not having gotten the guy." And for having let his defenses down because of his feelings for her. He hadn't been alert. He'd made a rookie blunder.

Agents were trained to never let the outside world take focus away from the job. But that was what he'd done. He'd let thoughts and emotions cloud his mind, dulling his senses. He was fortunate his failure this time hadn't resulted in harm to the civilian.

And that was how he needed to think of Alicia. She was a civilian and it was his job to protect her. Falling in love with her compromised his objective. He needed to be replaced and would make the request as soon as he could speak to Max.

Leaving Settler's Valley and Alicia was the best thing for them all.

THIRTEEN

Alicia sighed. There he went again. Taking the blame for something out of his control. Sunlight slanted through the windows and bathed the hospital room in a warm glow, but did nothing to dispel the gloom lurking at the edges of her mind.

Leo had nearly been killed last night. The thought tore her up inside. He looked so vulnerable lying there in the hospital bed, a stark white bandage wrapped around his head, and beneath the dressing, she knew, were stitches and bruises.

His green eyes were troubled with dark circles beneath and his jaw was stubbled with an emerging dark blond beard. His khakis and polo shirt, which seemed to be such a part of who he was, had been removed and replaced with a hospital gown. A lightweight blanket covered his legs to his chest.

Tenderness rose within her as she gripped his hand in her own. "Stop it. This is not your fault."

"But it is." Hardening his jaw, he looked away from her. "He ambushed me. I should have been more alert."

"Listen to me," she implored. "*Ambushed*, by the very nature of the word, means he lay in wait to attack you by surprise. How on earth could you have been prepared for that?"

"I should have taken True with me."

"Maybe, but then what if he'd incapacitated you both before he reached the house?"

Leo's gaze snapped back to her. The color drained from his face. "He reached the house?"

"Nearly." A shiver at the memory of the previous night's terror snaked down her spine. "But True alerted and then attacked him. I'm pretty sure Garry Pike is sporting a few bite marks right now."

Leo's teeth ground together. "At least True did his job."

"Enough," she said, letting some of her annoyance at his insistence of flogging himself bleed through her tone. "You need to rest and get better."

"I feel like I was run over by a semi," he groaned.

"Hit with a tire iron is more like it. The police found one discarded by Dad's old Chevy truck." The thing had had Leo's blood on it. "Chief Jarrett has everyone combing the county for Pike. He can't stay hidden for long."

The fierce determination on Leo's face had her tensing. "Then I better get up and get you somewhere safe until Max and Julianne return." He attempted to sit up again.

Placing her hands on his biceps, she gently pushed him back. "Oh, no, you don't. You're staying put."

He resisted her effort to keep him from getting up, but she was experienced at wrestling an active three-year-old into submission. She wasn't about to let this hunk of a man best her. "Look, I'm safe. I have a huge shadow who goes by the name of Officer Dorset. And your team returned in the wee hours of the morning."

Leo relaxed back and she straightened.

"Okay, good," he said. "I'll have to thank Chief Jarrett."

She couldn't keep from smiling. Ever the polite and well-mannered agent. "Your boss is in the hall wanting to speak to you. I made him wait until I knew for sure you were up to it. And Julianne is at the house with Charlie and Dad and the dogs."

Leo blinked as a resolute expression settled on his handsome face. Then he nodded. "Perfect. I need to talk to him."

"I don't want you to upset yourself unduly," she said, not trusting that he wouldn't try to get up again. "You need to rest and to heal."

He gave her a wary glance. "How long am I expected to be here?"

"The doctor wants to observe you for forty-eight hours."

"*Two days!* I can't stay here that long."

She'd thought that much time was a bit excessive, too, and had said as much to the physician. "The doctor said he'd reevaluate his opinion in twelve hours."

His jaw firmed. "I'd like to talk to Max now."

She left his side and stuck her head out the door. Max paced the hall, looking imposing in his uniform. He saw her and strode toward the room. Before she let him in, she said, "He needs to stay calm, okay?"

Max's clear blue eyes assessed her with mild surprise mingled with some amusement. Alicia felt a blush work its way up her neck. She was mothering Leo, but at the moment he needed someone to take care of him. And the truth was, she *wanted* to take care of him. She'd figure out how later.

"Okay," he said, his deep voice smooth. "I will take that under advisement."

She stepped aside so he could enter then followed him into the room. Leo's gaze pinned her to the floor.

"Would you mind letting us have the room?" Leo asked her.

Trying not to be hurt by the dismissal, she smiled tightly. "I'll go get coffee. Agent West, would you like a cup?"

"No, thank you," Max answered.

"Make sure Officer Dorset accompanies you," Leo instructed.

His concern softened her hurt a bit at being sent from the room. "Of course."

As soon as the door closed behind Alicia, Leo met Max's curious gaze. "You need to assign another agent to protect Alicia. In fact, Julianne is perfect for the job."

Max stroked his chin. "Really? Let me remind you, you volunteered for this job."

"Now I'm unvolunteering for it."

Max's mouth lifted at the corner in a mocking way that grated on Leo's nerves. "Too much for you to handle, huh?"

"What? No. It's just—I almost failed her. That creep got too close. Someone, anyone, will do a better job of protecting her and her family than me."

Max pulled a chair from the corner next to the bed and sat. His piercing blue gaze showed he wasn't the least bit amused. "No. I'm not taking you off this case. But we do need a new strategy."

Leo's stomach sank. "You agree with me, then, that I'm falling down on the job."

"Don't put words in my mouth, Gallagher," Max snapped. "I'm saying we need to stop waiting for him to show himself. We need to go hunting."

Under different circumstances, Leo would be on

board. "You've been showing his picture all over the place with no results," he pointed out.

"Correct. But he showed up last night and left traces of himself behind. We have highly trained dogs with us. Granted, each dog has a specific specialty, but I know the trainers have worked with them on tracking and air search. I have every confidence one of them will pick up this guy's scent and track him down."

Excited anticipation accelerated Leo's heart rate. Max was correct. The two trainers at the FBI Tactical K-9 Unit's headquarters had trained all the dogs in multiple disciplines beyond each dog's primary expertise.

True was trained in air search as well as water-detection rescues. Thunder used scent tracking in evidence recovery and Opal used scent tracking for bomb and explosive detection as well as drug and tactical detection.

The same principles applied in tracking a human on land. "You're right. Though one of us will have to stay with Alicia." She was his primary concern.

Max dropped his chin and stared at him. "Uh, you'll be staying here in the hospital. Julianne will stay with Ms. Duncan and her family while I track this guy."

Leo shook his head and ignored the pounding behind his eyes. "No way, Max. You're not going alone. Call in Ian or Tim."

"Ian is in Chicago attempting to interview Reginald and Esme Dupree's other sister, Violetta Dupree, and it would take too long for Tim to arrive. I need to hit the trail before it goes cold."

"I'm coming with you," Leo said. He forced himself to sit up.

Rising to his feet, Max pressed his lips into a thin,

hard line. "I'm ordering you to stand down, Agent. Or rather, lie back down."

Ignoring the request, Leo removed the IV and chest probes a second time. Only this time, he quickly shut off the irritating beeping machine. "You'll have to fire me. And even then you won't be able to stop me from doing what I need to do. You know you'd do the same thing."

After a long silent moment, Max held his hands up in surrender and stepped back, allowing Leo space to stand. He gestured toward the closed door. "Alicia is not going to like this," he said with something in his tone that sounded suspiciously like amusement.

"She'll get over it." Leo hoped. He went to the closet looking for his clothes. He found two bags, one filled with his uniform and the other containing his holster but not his sidearm. "Where's my gun?"

"Locked up," Max responded as he retook his seat. "If you're coming, get a move on."

"You're not going to fire me?"

"No, but I'm going to have a good time watching you tell Alicia what's going on when she comes back," he said, crossing one foot over his knee.

With his gut twisting into a knot, Leo went into the bathroom and put on his uniform. He stared at himself in the mirror. He needed a shave and a haircut. He touched the bandage around his head. The skin peeking out beneath the edge was purple. He looked horrible. No less than he deserved.

A hard, insistent knocking sounded at the bathroom door.

He took a bracing breath, because he knew without a doubt who was demanding his attention. He opened the door and found himself facing Alicia's fiery, pale blue—

eyed gaze. She looked so lovely standing there in her jeans and floral blouse with her strong, capable hands planted firmly on her hips. Her dark hair hung loose about her shoulders, making him itch to lift the strands from her neck and kiss the soft skin beneath.

She blinked at him and her mouth opened and closed several times before she blurted, "Are you crazy? Why are you dressed?"

"Because I have a job to do." He brushed past her, not liking the way her ire made him feel like he was in the wrong. He was doing this for her. To finally put an end to this nightmare she was living. So they could both go back to their lives. He could continue the search for Jake. And Alicia and her family would be able to relax and breathe easier knowing the killer was behind bars.

"You're supposed to be resting and letting that thick head of yours heal," she retorted hotly.

He stopped and turned to face her. "I need to do this, Alicia. I don't need your permission."

Her eyes narrowed. She turned to Max, who watched with suppressed laughter evident on his face.

"You." She pointed her finger at him. "You're his boss. Tell him he can't go."

Max held up his hands. "I tried. But like you said, he's got a thick head."

"And stubborn, too," she muttered.

Hating that he was putting her through this, he took her hand. "Please, Alicia. You have nothing to worry about."

"You suffered a head injury. There's plenty to worry about," she said.

Frustration pounded at his temples. Her concern warmed his heart. He wanted to kiss the worry from her brow and distract her from any fear she might harbor for his safety.

It was her safety that mattered.

They were wasting time arguing. The trail was growing cold with every passing second. It was time to leave. "I'm not your responsibility."

The hurt spreading across her face couldn't have made him feel any worse. Everything inside of him wanted to apologize, tell her how much her concern meant to him, how much *she* meant to him.

But he wouldn't. Couldn't.

Not if he hoped to make a clean break when the time came. He had to steel himself against his need to pull her to him. Instead, he said, "We need to roll. Now."

Alicia drew herself up and stared him down. "Fine. Let's go." She marched out the hospital-room door.

Max unfolded himself from the chair and clapped Leo on the back. "That went nicely, don't you think?"

Leo clenched his teeth together. When had his life become so complicated?

Alicia fumed as she sat in the SUV next to Officer Dorset, behind Leo, where she had a perfect view of his bandaged head. Stubborn, ornery, pigheaded man!

He was risking his health, for what? To catch a criminal because he was too proud to step aside and let others do what was necessary. Though she admired his commitment to his career and even respected his need to complete his mission—he was a man of integrity and honor, after all—she hated that he would put the job ahead of his own well-being.

When they arrived at the ranch, Leo opened her door and held out his hand. For a second she wanted to refuse to take it, but that would be childish. And would make it seem like she cared too much about him. Which she did, but he didn't need to know that.

So she slipped her hand into his and let him help her out of the SUV. His firm grasp and the pressure of their palms together made her want to hang on indefinitely and never let him go. That he held on a little longer than he needed to confused her.

Was he feeling the same pull to her as she felt toward him?

She searched his inscrutable gaze. What was he thinking? Did he care for her more than just as a person he was assigned to protect?

She wanted so badly to ask. To tell him she'd fallen for him. Instead, she broke away and headed quickly to the house, fighting back tears. She needed to be grounded in what was real. In what mattered most. Her son.

Not a too-perplexing man with gorgeous green eyes and mega control issues.

Leo watched Alicia's retreating back as pain spread through his chest. He'd hurt her, angered her and probably doused any feeling she had for him. But hadn't that been his intent? Yes, but that didn't mean he had to like it.

"Let's suit up. Then we'll get the dogs ready," Max said as he opened the back of his SUV.

Nodding, Leo went to his SUV, where he had his flak vest and more ammo. After the barn fire, he'd stored his assault rifle back into its compartment in the trunk. He retrieved the weapon.

Julianne came out of the house with all three dogs in tow and hurried over.

Leo went down on one knee to greet True, who lavished his face with wet kisses.

Opal trotted over to Max for a greeting.

"What's wrong with Alicia?" Julianne asked Max.

Though Leo couldn't see the two, he heard the concern in her voice and winced. He was the one responsible. He'd made Alicia upset enough that Julianne had noticed.

"See for yourself," Max answered.

A second later Julianne was standing over Leo with her hands on her hips. "What are you doing here? Shouldn't you be in the hospital?"

Leo ground his back teeth and rose. He couldn't handle another female scolding him. "Let it go, Julianne."

She turned to Max. "Explain."

He arched an eyebrow. "I didn't want to fire him."

Leo watched the exchange with wry amusement. The two worked well together.

He wasn't sure what either one's past was like, but he knew he trusted both Max and Julianne with his life. And with the lives of those he'd come to care about. His gaze went to the house.

Keep them safe, Lord. He sent up the silent plea then went back to the task of gearing up.

"What's the plan?" Julianne asked as she reached for her flak vest.

"I need you and Thunder to stay here with Ms. Duncan and her family," Max replied. "Leo and I will take the dogs out to track Garry Pike."

Julianne slanted Leo a glance. "He's okay enough to do that?"

"Yes, I am," Leo answered. He had to be.

She pursed her lips. "Aren't you on pain meds?"

"Nothing stronger than over-the-counter headache

medicine." He'd refused to take the stuff the doctor had offered because he hadn't wanted to muddle his mind.

Julianne sniffed. "No wonder Alicia's upset."

Leo didn't respond. What could he say? He knew Alicia didn't approve of what he was doing. Apparently, neither did Julianne. But he wouldn't let that stop him.

Once Leo, Max and the two dogs were properly out-fitted with bulletproof vests labeled with the FBI acronym, Leo led True to the porch around the house. Max and Opal followed. Leo could see the scuff marks and the dark stains in the dirt where True had drawn blood by biting Garry Pike.

"Get a good sniff of that," he told True. The dog put his nose to the ground and growled, no doubt remembering the scuffle he'd had last night with Pike.

Max allowed Opal to also sniff the area.

When he was sure True had a good feel for Pike's odor, Leo crouched down next to True. Unhooking True's leash, Leo said, "Search."

True lifted his nose to the sky and breathed in, his chest expanding. He put his nose to the ground and shuffled back and forth, moving away from the house for a hundred feet. Max let out Opal's fifty-foot lead so she could cover the area with her nose. Since she wasn't air-scent trained, he needed to keep her on leash, unlike True, who worked better and faster off leash.

True let out a series of barks indicating he'd caught the scent, and then he took off and ran toward the fence that separated the east side of the pasture from the ranch house.

"Here we go." Leo ran after True, praying the canine would lead him to the killer threatening Alicia.

FOURTEEN

Alicia tucked Charlie in for a midmorning nap. For a moment, she stood in the doorway watching her sweet little boy curl onto his side. His drowsy eyes fluttered closed and he sighed as he fell asleep.

Last night had been traumatic for them all. Dad and Charlie had hardly slept once she'd left with Leo in the ambulance.

She'd been so scared that Leo would die. So scared she wouldn't have an opportunity to tell him how much she'd come to care for him. She'd intended to tell him this morning, but then he went and checked himself out of the hospital against doctor's orders like a madman.

She blew out a frustrated breath, closed Charlie's door and headed back downstairs, where Julianne and her father were drinking coffee at the dining table. Thunder sat by the door and the puppy slept nearby. Alicia grabbed a mug, poured herself some coffee and joined them.

"Miss Julianne was just telling me about Billings, Montana," Dad said. "It sounds like a nice place."

"It's a city, Dad," Alicia commented. "You don't care for cities."

Dad stared into his cup. "Hmm. True. I do prefer the wide-open spaces of the ranch. But it might be interesting to go to art galleries, museums and movie theaters without having to drive several hours."

She'd never heard her dad talk like this before. "What's brought this on?"

"I'm just babbling." He rose and washed out his cup before putting it in the sink. "Don't mind me. I'm going to go check on the horses."

Confused, she watched him leave the house. Chalking up her dad's strange behavior to the drama of the last few days, she sighed and sipped from her cup before turning her attention to the woman across from her. "Thank you for being here."

Julianne smiled. "My pleasure."

"Really? You wouldn't rather be out there with the guys hunting down the criminal?"

Julianne laughed. "Yes, truth be told, I would, but this is where I'm needed."

Liking her honesty, Alicia asked, "Have you worked with Leo long?"

"A few years," the agent replied with a kind smile. "He's a really good guy. Not normally so bullheaded."

Annoyance bubbled in Alicia's tummy. She pictured the stubborn set of his jaw. "It makes me so mad that he's out there. He should be lying down and resting. He could trip and fall and do even more damage. He—" She cut herself off from the litany of reasons why Leo shouldn't be out searching for Garry Pike right now.

"Men." Julianne shook her head with a rueful grin. "Sometimes I think they are truly an alien species."

"Yes." Alicia liked Julianne. Needing to think of

something other than Leo, she asked, "Are you from Billings?"

"No." She examined her coffee cup. "East Texas."

"I've never been to that part of Texas," Alicia said. "Is your family still there?"

Julianne shook her head. "No. Unfortunately, they are both gone now."

Empathy made Alicia reach a hand across the table and touch the agent's hand. "I'm sorry."

"Thank you."

Easing back, Alicia asked, "What made you go into law enforcement?"

Sadness entered the agent's dark eyes. "A combination of things. My grandfather was an officer. I wanted to be like him. During college, a friend went missing. She was never seen again. I felt so helpless at the time. I decided I wanted to do something with my life to honor her, something to make a difference in the lives of other missing persons, so I applied to the FBI. Somehow Thunder and I found each other, and well, here we are."

"That's very noble."

Julianne gave a self-effacing smile. "It's fulfilling."

"That's how I feel about teaching and motherhood. Being with kids makes me happy. Once Charlie is old enough, I'll go back to teaching. After his father's death, I felt like I needed to be home with my son."

"And I, for one, appreciate people like you. The thought of a room full of children scares me more than a gunfight."

Overhead, there was a bump on the floor. Charlie must be awake. Alicia sighed. He didn't nap very long.

Julianne's phone buzzed. She glanced at the caller display panel. "Dylan. I need to take this." She rose and took her call outside. The dogs followed her outside.

Figuring she should go check on Charlie, Alicia went upstairs. Charlie's door was ajar; he must have gotten up to use the restroom. Hopefully he was back in bed now.

She pushed the door open. The bed came into view. Charlie was exactly as she'd left him, curled on his side, fast asleep. Tenderness swelled beneath her breastbone.

The creak of the rocking chair in the corner startled her. She whipped her gaze toward the chair and confronted the cold-eyed stare of Garry Pike, holding a gun aimed at her.

"How did you get in here?" With Herculean effort, Alicia kept her voice hushed so she wouldn't wake Charlie. The last thing she needed was to scare him. Her pulse pounded in her ears and panic had a stranglehold on her to the point that she felt dizzy.

There was no way of escaping. He'd either shoot her or shoot Charlie. She stepped to the side, in front of Charlie's bed so that she blocked Garry Pike's line of sight to her son.

From his place in the rocking chair in the corner, Garry sneered. "The same way we're leaving."

Her stomach turned. She was going to throw up, but she had to stay in control of her fear if she wanted to live. "Fine. Let's go."

Garry stood, towering over her. "Grab your kid and then we'll go."

"No!" She drew herself up to her full five foot ten inches, but she still had to crane her neck to look at his face. His cold, dark eyes sent a chill slithering along her limbs. "He'll just slow you down. He didn't see you. He can't identify you. Leave him out of this." She needed to get this man away from Charlie.

After a heartbeat, Garry's mouth twisted. "I'll come back and kill him if you don't cooperate."

Though his threat caused a spurt of terror, she was grateful he'd relented on taking Charlie with them. "I'll cooperate."

At least until she had the opportunity to get away.

He waved his gun, motioning for her to leave the room. With one last longing glance at her son, she walked out of the room, praying she'd see Charlie again.

She headed toward the staircase, hoping Julianne would have come back inside from her phone call or that Thunder would sense the danger. But the K-9 and the puppy had followed Julianne outside.

Before she'd taken a few steps, Garry yanked her by the arm. "This way," he hissed.

He led her to her bedroom. The balcony door stood open. He pushed her out onto the balcony. A rope ladder had been attached to the railing. She glanced around, searching for Officer Dorset, but there was no sign of him.

She looked out toward the horse pasture but Dad and the horses weren't in view. Had Garry done something to her father? She sent up a plea to God that wasn't the case. Fear squeezed her lungs. She could scream. Julianne would hear her and come to her aid.

But then he'd go back inside and harm her son before the agent could reach them. She couldn't do anything to put Charlie in jeopardy.

"Climb down," Garry told her. When she hesitated, he added, "It'd be nothing to shoot you now and then go back for your kid. If you try to run, I'll shoot your son." He voiced her thoughts, making her glad she hadn't acted.

"All right. I'm going." She carefully climbed down. When her feet hit the earth, she glanced up. Garry was already halfway to the ground and still had the gun trained on her.

He jumped the last few feet, landing easily. With a flick of his beefy arm, the rope ladder unhooked from the railing and sailed silently down to land in the dirt beside him. He gathered the rope with his free hand, tucked it under his arm then grabbed her by the wrist and dragged her with him toward the equipment barn.

Thinking he intended to kill her there, she prayed for a quick death. Her heart sobbed with sorrow and grief. She wouldn't be there to watch her son grow up. She wouldn't ever have the chance to tell Leo how she felt. She'd missed her opportunity for happiness.

Garry steered her around the building and across the expanse of wildflowers toward the road. Once there, he led her to a discarded pile of cottonwoods that had been cleared from the back pasture and still needed to be hauled away. The debris hid two huge boulders.

Now that they were away from the house, she had to escape. She eyed a large branch sticking out of the debris.

"Come on—this way," he commanded, pulling her behind the boulders.

Surprise washed over her to see the black muscle car that had tried to ram into her car. If she got in that car, she was as good as dead. Now was her opportunity to strike and try to get away.

With a sharp twist, she broke from his grasp and lunged for the branch. Her hands wrapped around the rough bark.

Garry grabbed a handful of her dark hair and yanked

her backward. She brought the branch with her, swinging at him. She heard a satisfying thump before his fist smashed into her face and the world went dark.

"This is where he was camping out," Max said as he toed the remains of a fire in a makeshift pit.

Leo stared at the site, where a bedroll had been neatly placed beneath the branches of a silver sagebrush tree. Garry Pike had been hiding out three miles from the ranch house. There was a plastic bag tied to a branch filled with garbage. A cooler was tucked at the base of the tree filled with edibles and water bottles.

The two dogs sniffed the ground, padding around as they tried to capture Pike's scent to determine which direction he'd gone from here. Every so often True lifted his nose to the air, his head bobbing back and forth to catch the wind.

True moved south, farther and farther away from the campsite. Leo kept pace with his canine. Max and Opal followed. A mile later they came to the main road leading to and from Settler's Valley.

True let out a loud bark and took off down the road. Leo whistled, bringing True up short. The dog whirled around and raced back to sit at Leo's side. Leo hooked the leash to his collar. He wasn't about to endanger his partner by letting him loose near a road.

"Lead the way," Max said.

Letting True's lead out enough that the canine could work, but not so far that Leo wouldn't be able to pull him out of harm's way if a car passed by, they moved along the road for another half mile or so.

"We're going in a circle," Leo stated impatiently as he followed True back to the Howard ranch's driveway. Why was the chocolate Lab leading them back to where they'd started? Dread itched at Leo's nape. He quickened his steps.

Max grunted in acknowledgment.

Not far from the entrance to the Howard ranch drive, the dogs alerted on a massive pile of debris that had been heaped on the side of the road. It looked like cuttings from several trees had been stacked on top of two large boulders.

Using caution, Leo and Max ventured closer to inspect the sight. There were tire tracks in the soft dirt disappearing behind the boulders. Though the space was empty, Leo now knew where Garry Pike had hidden his muscle car and why the Settler's Valley police hadn't found it. But where was Garry now?

If he were out driving his car, he would be spotted easily enough. It wasn't like there was more than one dark-colored, high-performance vehicle roaming the highways and byways of Settler's Valley, Wyoming.

True's nose twitched. He pulled at the leash, forcing Leo away from the scene. The dog clearly wanted to run down the highway. Leo could only assume Garry had taken off in that direction.

Max's cell phone rang.

"West," Max answered. He listened while the person on the other side of the call talked. Leo could tell by the grimness darkening his boss's expression that something was wrong.

It was a full minute before Max asked, "How long ago? We're heading back now." He hung up.

Heart beating erratically in his chest, Leo asked, "What's happening?"

"Alicia's missing."

Leo staggered beneath the oppressive weight of that statement. "How? Where's Officer Dorset? Julianne? She was supposed to be guarding her. And what about Charlie?" He began to run toward the ranch house.

Max and the dogs kept pace with Leo. "Charlie's safe. Julianne found Dorset tied up inside the equipment barn. Mr. Howard was with the horses and didn't see anything. Julianne had stepped outside to take a call from Dylan. Thunder and the puppy found a raw steak and were distracted. We'll hear the rest when we get there."

A planned abduction. Increasing his speed, Leo forced his legs to work as he fought back the throbbing in his head. He'd failed her again. Only this time was so much worse. Garry had managed to snatch her.

Leo shouldn't have left her. He should have arranged for an army to stand watch. This one man shouldn't be so hard to find and apprehend. But then again, a lone operator was always more tricky to capture.

And from everything he'd read on Pike, the man was a chameleon, able to move about undetected for years while doing his criminal activities.

Julianne and Howard came out of the house. Officer Dorset sat on the stairs rubbing his head.

Howard's face was pale. Leo flinched at the panic in the older man's eyes.

"I stepped out for just a moment," Julianne explained. "When I returned, I thought Alicia had gone upstairs to check on Charlie. But after a while when she didn't come back down, I went up to search for her. She's gone. There's a balcony off the master bedroom. I can only guess that somehow Pike gained access to the house from there."

"You have to find her," Howard said, his voice shaking.

"Where's Charlie?" Leo asked.

"He's still asleep," Julianne said.

"You stay here for when he wakes up," Max instructed. "Leo and I are going after Pike and Ms. Duncan. Officer Dorset, you come with us. Call your chief."

"Already have," Dorset responded. "He's got everyone looking for Pike." The younger officer grimaced. "I'm so sorry I let you down. He came out of nowhere and clobbered me good."

"He seems to do that," Max said drily.

To Howard, Leo asked, "I need something of Alicia's for the dogs to smell."

"I'll get her sweater," Howard said. "It's hanging just inside the door." He shuffled off faster than Leo would have expected.

He returned a few minutes later with Alicia's sweater. Leo took it and held it out for the dogs to sniff. Then he and Max loaded the dogs into Max's SUV. With Max driving, Leo in the front passenger seat and Officer Dorset in the backseat, they headed toward town with the windows down. True and Opal shared one window.

Leo gripped the door handle until his knuckles turned white. His other hand curled into a fist and pounded his thigh.

"What do we know about Pike?" Max asked.

Focusing on Max, Leo tumbled the question through his mind. "He works for Dupree. He's killed two women that we know of. He dumped both bodies in the river. Two more are missing." He paused as it struck him where to go. "The marina. Head to the marina."

"Good thinking," Max said and turned at the next intersection toward the marina. When they reached the gravel parking lot, Max brought the SUV to a screeching halt. Leo jumped out and scanned the area.

There. In the back corner was the black muscle car. It had to be Pike's. Adrenaline surged through Leo. After grabbing his assault rifle, he released True and held out Alicia's sweater for True to smell again.

"Hey, that was fast," a rotund man said as he ambled up. "I just clicked off with the police department. They said they'd send someone right over."

Max came around the vehicle. "Sir, what's the problem?"

"Some lunatic and his girl just stole my boat," he exclaimed.

"That had to be Pike with Alicia." Leo could only imagine how terrified Alicia had to be. "Was the woman all right?"

The man made a face. "She was sporting a nasty bruise on her face. That fellow probably smacked her good."

Rage erupted in Leo's belly. Pike had hit Alicia. Leo's fingers curled into fists. He couldn't wait to get his hands on Pike and return the favor.

"We'll secure a boat and head upstream," Max told Leo.

"That will take too long," Leo argued. "You get the boat. True and I will find her faster on ground along the shore."

Max nodded. "I want him alive, Leo. We need whatever information he has on Dupree and Jake."

Despite wanting the same thing as his boss, if it came down to Alicia or Pike, there was no contest. Alicia would win. "I can't make that promise."

Fingers curling into fists around the sweater in his

hands, Leo bent to eye level with True and looked into his soulful dark brown eyes. His chocolate coat gleamed in the sunshine. He sat up straight and proud, ready to work. "Find Alicia."

The dog blinked as if he understood.

Leo unhooked the leash and True ran toward the water. Leo worked hard to keep up, or at least keep the dog in sight. True reached the water then veered left along the shore, crashing through bushes, speeding over rocks and river debris with sure-footed confidence.

Leo slipped and slid in his heavy boots. His head throbbed with each step but he didn't care. He only cared about finding Alicia. Having to split his focus between where he was stepping and keeping an eye on the river, along with making sure he didn't lose sight of True, was taxing his brain. The dull ache he'd been trying to ignore roared. He gritted his teeth together, knowing he would be adding a sore jaw to his list of ailments once this was over.

His heart beat too fast, pumping blood with alarming speed. His limbs felt on fire. Sweat broke out on his neck. He had to find Alicia before it was too late.

"Lord, please, I beg of You, show us where to find her. Lead us to Alicia. Make Pike stop whatever he's doing or intending to do. Give me the strength, the courage, to face this trial. In Jesus's name, amen," he said. Fear and panic crowded for prominence in his mind.

True's frantic barking jerked Leo's focus to finding the dog. True had discovered something and was alerting his partner, the constant barking leading him to True's location. Leo fought his way through the thick underbrush and tight growing trees and broke through at the water's edge. He halted in the shadow of a tree, reluctant to show himself. He didn't want to force Pike to act.

In the middle of the deepest part of the river, about a hundred and fifty yards away from shore, not far from the place where Pike had dumped the first Esme look-alike, was a motorized fishing boat idling in the water.

Alicia sat on the port-side gunwale. Garry Pike stood behind her with a gun pressed against her temple.

FIFTEEN

The sound of a dog barking gave Alicia hope despite the fear trembling through her. She sat perched on the edge of the fishing boat Pike had stolen from the marina. Her feet dangled in the cold water, making her shiver.

Her fingers gripped the lip of the side, hanging on for dear life. Pike loomed behind her, the hard, round barrel of his pistol pressed into her temple.

The afternoon breeze whipped her hair into her face. The strands stuck to the tears streaming down her cheeks. She closed her eyes and sent up a silent prayer of protection.

She didn't want to die. She couldn't leave her son an orphan. She had to talk Pike out of killing her. She forced her voice to stay calm. "Please, you don't have to do this."

"But I do," he responded menacingly. "No loose ends. My boss will skin me alive if I let you live."

She opened her eyes and craned her neck back to look at him. His cold stare made her want to turn away but she held his gaze, forcing him to see her. "You work for Dupree, right? Help the FBI bring him down. Cooperate with them. I know they'd give you leniency."

"No way," he spit. "I'm no rat. Besides, the feds aren't going to do squat for me or to me."

He thought he was above the law. He couldn't be more wrong. "The FBI has your picture. They know who you are and what you've done. You've killed two women."

"A third is no big deal."

His smug smile angered her, tempering her fear enough to make her voice sharp. "Killing me will only make things worse for you."

"Maybe. But I'll enjoy it."

"Where are the other two women you kidnapped? Are they dead, too?"

His lip curled. "Naw. They're alive. For now."

She hated the menace in his tone that made it clear he had every intention of doing away with his other two hostages. "Where are they?"

Not that she was in a position to help them, but keeping him distracted might buy her some time. Give Leo a chance to find her. She sent up a silent plea that God would lead Leo and True to her.

"Upstream. But you shouldn't be concerned about them when it's your life I'm about to snuff out."

She couldn't take looking at his cruel face any longer. She faced forward in time to see True charge into the water up to his chest. His bark was ferocious. His lips were drawn back and his teeth bared. Her heart leaped. If True was here then so was Leo.

God had answered her prayer.

She searched the shore for the man she loved. There. In the shadows, she could just make out his form.

The sound of an approaching powerboat snagged her attention away from Leo. Officer Dorset drove the speedboat like an expert, and Max and Opal were beside the police officer.

She was being rescued.

Pike grabbed a handful of her hair and dragged her backward. Sharp pain made her yelp and grab at the hand fisted in her hair.

"Stand up," Pike ordered.

She scrambled to get her feet beneath her. The boat rocked with their movement, making it difficult to gain her balance. Her gaze went back to Leo. He'd disappeared, but True was still at the water's edge. His frantic barks ricocheted off the canyon walls. What was Leo doing? Where was he?

He wouldn't have left her.

She managed to get both feet flat on the floorboards of the boat.

The other speedboat slowed and came to a halt about twenty yards away. Officer Dorset drew his sidearm. Max cupped his hands around his mouth and yelled, "Give up, Pike. There's only one way this ends well. Let the woman go."

Pike let go of her hair and yanked on her arm, forcing her in front of him like a shield. "Let us go or the woman dies."

He was going to kill her no matter what. Wildly she looked back at the shore and caught a glint of sunlight reflecting off something in the trees. Leo? Had he climbed the tree and was now sitting on a branch with his assault rifle aimed at Pike?

She had to do something—anything—to give Leo a clear shot. Taking a deep breath, she let her knees go limp. Her sagging weight threw him off balance.

"Hey!" he screeched and tried to regain his hold on her.

Using all the strength she possessed in her legs, she exploded upward, ramming the back of her head into his nose. With a high-pitched cry, he released her. Without hesitating, she flung herself overboard into the water, hitting her head on the side of the boat.

She winced. The cold river stole her breath. As her head submerged beneath the surface, she heard the loud crack of gunfire chased by a burning pain.

Leo's heart stopped. He stared through the scope of his assault rifle and watched as Alicia went overboard. Pike fired into the water. Leo pulled the trigger. His aim was true. A kill shot. Pike crumpled to the floorboard of the boat.

"True! Rescue!" Leo shouted as he scrambled off the limb of the tree he'd climbed. He didn't wait to see if True obeyed. Leo had every confidence the dog would do what he'd been trained to do. Opal's deep bark bounced off the water.

Leo swung down from the branch and jumped to the ground, taking the force of the landing with bent knees. He'd barely hit the dirt before he was running toward the water, slipping the strap to his rifle across his chest. Then he charged into the river. Ahead of him, True swam toward the spot where Alicia had disappeared.

Please, don't let her drown, Lord. He still couldn't believe she'd acted so valiantly and brilliantly. He'd seen her crumple then jerk upright to bash the back of her head into Pike's face before she'd thrown herself into the water. Her actions had given Leo a wide-open shot. But had she paid the ultimate price for her bravery?

His gut twisted and he pushed himself harder, to

swim faster. They had to reach her before her lungs filled with water.

Max and Dorset had tethered their boat to the fishing boat. Max boarded the other boat and checked Pike's vitals. Leo wasn't surprised when Max shook his head. Pike had shot into the water, at Alicia. There was only one course of action for Leo to take.

True dived beneath the water. Leo was almost there. The dog popped back to the surface, dragging Alicia with him. He had a mouthful of her shirt. She appeared unconscious. Her dark hair floated on the water. Leo kicked harder and reached them.

"Here," Max shouted and threw two orange seat cushions into the water.

Leo grabbed one flotation device then hooked an arm around Alicia and drew her to his chest. True let go of Alicia's shirt and latched on to the other cushion.

Blood matted the side of Alicia's head. Fear that she'd been shot grabbed Leo by the lungs and squeezed. Kicking hard to move them closer to the speedboat, he forced himself to stay calm and in control. He checked her breathing by putting his ear close to her nose and mouth. "She's not breathing!"

Officer Dorset and Max helped to pull her in and laid her on the bottom of the boat. Leo boosted True into the boat before he hefted himself in. He stripped off his rifle and set it aside. Opal greeted True and barked as the canine shook the water from his coat, spraying the other dog.

Max had Alicia turned on her side to keep any water in her mouth and nose from going down to her lungs. Leo nudged Max aside to check Alicia for a pulse. There was one. Yes!

He laid her flat and performed rescue breathing by pressing the heel of one hand to her forehead and pushing her head back to open her airway. Then he pinched her nostrils together, turned her face toward him and sealed his mouth over hers and gave her four strong breaths.

She jerked and gasped. He backed away and rolled her to her side as she coughed and spit out river water, then took hiccuping gulps of air. His relief that she was alive nearly overwhelmed him. Tears of joy burned at the backs of his eyes. He stared in her pretty pale face. She gazed up at him, looking a bit disoriented. Love flooded his chest. He smoothed back her hair, careful not to disturb the wound to her head. "Hey, sweet lady."

Panic flared in her blue eyes. "Pike?"

"You never have to worry about him again," he told her. "I promise."

"You always keep your promises." She sighed and melted into his arms. "God answered my prayers. He sent you to find me."

"That He did."

There was a gash on her right biceps. From Pike's bullet? Leo was sure the thug had only managed to discharge one round. Why did she have two wounds?

He gingerly gathered her close and became aware that two other boats had stopped. Chief Jarrett jumped aboard the speedboat. Anxiety deepened the lines around his eyes and made his voice shake. "Is she okay?"

"She'll live," Leo told him. "But we need to get her to the hospital."

Complications from the water exposure could result in pneumonia or infection. They needed to make sure her lungs were clear and the wounds she'd suffered were cleaned and dressed. He prayed there would be no more life-threatening situations for the lovely widow.

"Officer Dorset will take you to the marina," Jarrett said. "An ambulance will be waiting."

Around them Max and the chief went about securing the scene.

Guilt scrubbed at Leo like sandpaper. He met Alicia's gaze. "I'm so sorry this happened to you. I failed you."

Her dark winged eyebrows drew together. "No. You saved me. You came after me. I'm so grateful."

He didn't want her gratitude; he wanted her love but had no right to ask for it. So instead, he lightly touched his lips to hers in a tender kiss.

When the speedboat reached the marina, the ambulance was waiting just as Chief Jarrett had promised.

He explained to the paramedics what had happened as they loaded Alicia onto a stretcher and wheeled her toward the back bay of the emergency vehicle.

"Come with me?" Her eyes implored him and she held his hand tightly in hers. "You're hurt, too."

"Minor stuff." Nothing he couldn't handle or that couldn't be treated later.

"I'll be there as soon as I can," he assured her. Although every cell in his body wanted to go with her right then and there, he had a job to finish. He would have to give a statement. There would be an investigation in an officer-involved shooting. He knew it was a clean incident. He'd had no choice. "I'll let your family know what's happened."

Releasing his hand, she nodded. "Thank you."

The doors to the ambulance closed with a resounding thud that reverberated within his chest.

* * *

"Mommy!" Charlie's exuberant cry brought tears of happiness to Alicia. He ran into the hospital room, followed by her dad. She lay propped up on a hospital bed, her head and arm bandaged. She was now dry and warm but the shivers hadn't abated yet.

After the ambulance had whisked her away from the river, she'd been admitted to the hospital and put through a series of tests to determine if there were any other injuries besides the two visible ones. As far as the doctors could tell, she was fine.

Her head now sported two stitches and her right biceps four. The head wound was from hitting the side of the boat as she'd gone in the water; the other injury was where Pike's bullet grazed her arm.

With her uninjured arm, she hugged her son close, relishing the feeling of him against her, and smiled at her dad. She was surprised to see tears in his eyes. He came to her side and kissed her forehead beneath the bandage.

"Hi, sweetheart. We've come to bring you home," he announced. "Leo is waiting at the entrance with that amazing dog of his."

Her heart sputtered. She'd been half-afraid Leo would leave without saying goodbye. "I'm ready to get out of here."

"Good." Dad's gaze pierced her. "Are you sure you're all right?"

"I am. These will heal quickly," she assured him, hating to see the worry in his eyes. "Thanks to Leo and True, this ordeal is over."

Dad gave a slow nod and a speculative gleam entered

his gaze. "Yes. We've all grown very fond of Agent Leo Gallagher."

She smiled, remembering his pronouncement that he was a keeper. Leo was certainly that. And she would like nothing better than to keep him close to her heart forever. "Yes, Dad, we have."

His face lit up. "I'm glad to hear it. I believe he's grown fond of us, too."

If only she knew what Leo's feelings were for sure.

"I'll light a fire under the doctor and get your discharge papers," Dad said and hustled from the room.

Charlie nestled into her embrace. "Agent Leo said you went into the river. Did you slip off the rock?"

She laughed with joy at her son's innocence. She wished she could capture him at this age and never let him grow up. "Something like that. What have you been doing?"

His little face beamed. "Miss Julianne and I played I Spy and we took the dogs for walks and we ate sherbet and watched Barney."

"She took good care of you, buddy." Alicia would be forever grateful to the agent. She hoped they would be able to stay in touch once she moved on to another assignment.

Thinking about the agents leaving brought an ache to her heart. She didn't want Leo to go. Everything inside of her rebelled at the idea of him not being a part of her and Charlie's lives.

But what was she supposed to do?

Even if she told him that she loved him, she could never ask him to give up his career and move to the ranch. She wouldn't want him to do that. He was a dedicated officer of the law who had proved to her he could also be a man who would devote himself to those he loved. But she couldn't leave the ranch. Her dad needed her.

On the other hand, Billings, Montana, was only two hours away. Close enough that if Dad needed something she could come back. She and Charlie could come back on the weekends and holidays. They could hire some teens to come and help Dad with the chores around the ranch. The more she thought about the logistics, the more conceivable she found the idea.

She mentally snorted. Of course, planning a life with Leo was a moot point if he didn't feel the same about her. If he wasn't interested in building a future that included her and Charlie.

Only one way to find out. She had to expose her heart and pray Leo loved her, too.

An hour later, Leo carried Alicia into the living room of the Howard ranch house. Charlie hovered close by waiting for the opportunity to be with his mother. According to Julianne, Charlie had been scared when he'd awoken to discover his mother not there. He'd told the agent that he'd had bad dreams that a bad man had taken his mommy away.

Apparently he hadn't been completely asleep when Pike had kidnapped Alicia. Leo hoped the boy would forget whatever he'd seen or heard now that the danger had passed.

He bent to gently lower Alicia to the couch cushions. She hung on to him for a moment. Her arms around his neck were thrilling and her body so light in his arms.

"You're spoiling me," she murmured close to his ear,

her breath tickling the sensitive skin. "I could get used to being swept off my feet."

Her words bounced around his head and his heart. He'd like nothing better than to sweep her up and carry her off to some tropical paradise, where it would be just the two of them. But that wasn't going to happen. She may not blame him for failing to keep Pike away, but he certainly blamed himself.

And now that Alicia was safe, he had to let her go back to the life she had been leading before this nightmare came storming in to disturb her world. "You deserve to be swept off your feet."

He set her down. Her hands lingered on his arms as he drew away.

"Can we talk?" she asked in a low voice so that only he could hear.

Heart slamming against his ribs, he straightened. "Sure. But there's someone else here who needs your attention." He stepped aside so Charlie could climb onto the couch and snuggle against his mother's side. A place Leo wished to be but knew he didn't deserve.

Julianne and Max came downstairs with their to-go bags in hand.

"You leaving?" Leo asked.

"Yes," Max answered. "Need to get back to headquarters. Chief Jarrett has everything in hand here." He gestured to River. "We'll take the pup with us and hand him over to Thomas and Faith."

"Thank you." The two master trainers at headquarters would whip the pup into shape in no time. "His name is River, but I'd like to add Jake to his name."

Julianne bent to pet the puppy. "River Jake. I think

Jake would like that. In fact, we should all find puppies to bring into the fold in honor of Jake until he returns."

"Good idea," Max said. "When we get back to head-quarters we'll tell the others." He turned to Leo. "You should be cleared and ready to return to work by morning."

Leo knew that his boss was purposely giving him some time to say goodbye. Grateful, he inclined his head. "Thanks. True and I will head out at first light."

"After breakfast is soon enough. By the way, Ian called to say Violetta Dupree slammed the door in his face when he went to interview her," Max said. "I'm not sure we'll get any cooperation from that quarter."

"Too bad." Having both sisters testifying against their brother and uncle would have helped the FBI's case.

Max turned to Harmon and stuck out his hand. "Sir, it's been a pleasure. Let me know if there is anything else you need. The FBI Tactical K-9 Unit is at your disposal."

They shook hands. "Will do, Max. I appreciate your help."

Leo wondered what that was about. He remembered the way Max and Harmon had shut themselves up in the den. What had they been discussing?

Julianne gave Harmon a hug. "I hope to see you again soon."

"Me, too," the older man said, returning her hug.

Max stepped to the couch. "Alicia, it's been a pleasure even if the circumstances haven't been. Thank you for your hospitality."

"You're welcome, Agent West," Alicia replied. "And thank you for all you've done."

Julianne leaned in to hug Alicia and then Charlie. "I'll miss you two. Stay in touch, okay?"

"I'd like that," Alicia told her and hugged her back.

"Will you come back and play with me?" Charlie asked as he flung his arms around her neck.

"You bet, buddy." Julianne kissed the top of his head and then straightened. She looked at Leo. "This is a lovely family."

Confused by her words and the subtle message he was sure she was trying to convey, he nodded. "I'll see you tomorrow."

Max collected Opal and the puppy, while Julianne leashed up Thunder. The dogs seemed reluctant to leave as their handlers ushered them out the front door.

Alicia leaned her head against the backrest. "I think I'll close my eyes for just a moment. What about you, Charlie?"

The boy sighed and cuddled closer. "I can do that."

Harmon clapped a hand on Leo's back. "Why don't you come help me with the horses and we'll let these two rest."

Leo hated to let Alicia out of his sight, but now that the threat to her life was gone, he had no rational reason to refuse. "Sure. I can do that."

He followed Howard out of the house and to the pasture. As soon as they reached the gate, instead of opening it and calling the three horses, Howard turned to face him. "You're so eager to leave my daughter and grandson behind?"

Leo squared his jaw. His mind scrambled to make sense of what he was asking. "No. I mean, I have to leave."

"But you love my daughter," the older man stated with conviction.

The roar of blood pounding in his ears caused Leo to shake his head. "What? How did you—"

"It's obvious. I see the way you look at her. The care you take with her and Charlie. They love you, you know."

Leo blinked, digesting Harmon's words. "It is? They do?"

"Yes. What are you going to do about it?"

Leo ran a hand through his hair and leaned against the gate. Despair weighted down his shoulders. "Nothing. They deserve so much better than the likes of me."

Harmon scoffed. "Nonsense. You're a better man than I've come across in a long time. Your boss speaks highly of you and I've seen the kind of man you are with my own eyes. The only way you'll not deserve my daughter and grandson is if you walk away. They need you. And I suspect you need them." He opened the gate and whistled. "Now, let's get these horses fed and their hooves cleaned." He shuffled forward, grumbling, "I'm getting too old for this work."

Leo stared at the mountains rising in the distance. He did need Alicia and Charlie. With them by his side, could he finally be made whole?

After dinner, Alicia asked Dad to give Charlie a bath so she and Leo could talk. Nervous flutters danced a minuet in her tummy. She was about to lay her heart bare and open herself up to rejection by telling Leo how she felt. But the alternative, to let him leave in the morning without expressing her love for him, wasn't acceptable.

She wouldn't be able to live with herself if she didn't find the courage to confess her love.

As soon as Charlie and Dad disappeared into the downstairs bathroom, she patted the seat next to her on the couch. "Come sit by me."

Leo had insisted on cooking a delicious dinner of roasted chicken, savory rice and green beans. Apparently he'd stopped at the grocery store on his way to pick up her dad and Charlie. He'd cleaned up after dinner as well. Now he hung the drying cloth on the hook by the sink and strode over to the couch. He took a seat on the opposite end.

She frowned. Well, if the mountain wouldn't come to her… She slid across the leather surface until she was next to him. His eyebrows rose. She smiled and captured his hand. "I have something to say and I need you not to interrupt me."

His mouth twitched. "Okay."

"I know it's crazy, we've only known each other for a short time, but—" She faltered, her courage flagging.

"It's been an intense time," he interjected during her hesitation.

"Yes. But during this time I've realized several things. I've been too scared of being hurt to let anyone get close to me."

"That's understandable," he said softly.

She squeezed his hand. "I let you get close. And I know that doing so was the best thing I could have ever done. What—"

"I like being close to you."

She blinked at the interruption. "What I'm trying to say to you is—"

He slipped his hand from hers and cupped her face. "I've fallen in love with you."

Her mouth gaped open. "Hey, that was supposed to be my line." Then his words registered. "Wait. What? You've fallen in love with me?"

"Yes. Though I still have a hard time believing I could ever be the man you deserve, I want to try to be the man you need."

Her heart soared. She encircled her arms around his neck and drew him closer. "You're all I need. You and Charlie." She pressed her mouth to his, exploring in a caress of give-and-take. She loved this man with all her being.

Coming up for air, Leo said huskily, "I have to find Jake before I can make any permanent changes in my life."

She laid a hand over his heart. "I know." She wished she could take away the burden of guilt he felt for his friend's abduction. "We can work out the details of our lives later."

"Why wait?" Dad stood there grinning with a clean and giggling Charlie on his hip. "We should all move to Billings."

Alicia stared. "Dad, what about the ranch?"

"I've already listed the ranch with a Realtor," he said as he set Charlie on the floor. "And thanks to Max and his contacts, I've found a real nice place to live in Billings."

"So that's what you and Max were doing squirreled away in your office," Leo said. "I was wondering."

"Yep," her dad replied, looking pleased with himself. He looked at his daughter. "I didn't want to say anything to upset you, dear, but I just don't have the energy anymore to run the ranch. And you need to reclaim your life, not live mine."

Alicia winced. She hated to see her dad slowing down but she was glad that he had a plan, even if it meant giving up the ranch. "I guess we'll have to sell the horses." The thought made her sad.

"No," her dad said firmly. "Max had a friend who knew a lady… Anyway, we found a place we can board the horses just outside of town. It has great reviews online. I've talked to the owner and she seems like a lovely woman. A widow, about my age."

The twinkle in Dad's eyes filled the remaining empty spaces in Alicia's heart. Seemed they were all ready for a new start.

Charlie raced to the couch and squirmed his way on the couch between her and Leo. She glanced at Leo and was gratified to see the love shining in his eyes as he gazed at her son. He loved her and he loved Charlie.

Turning back to her father, she said, "Dad, I understand."

"It's time I made a change in my life." His gaze encompassed them all. "It's time we all made some changes."

Stunned, she faced Leo. Had he told her father how he felt? His smile made her heart melt. He lifted her hand and kissed her palm. "I agree."

Her pulse thumped. "Meaning?"

"I was hoping to do this in some romantic way but…" He slipped from the couch and went on one knee.

Her pulse skipped several beats. Her breath caught and held. Hope rose like a kite in a gust of wind, but she held on to the tail, afraid to let it soar.

"I know the timing of this is a bit out of the ordinary," he said. "A whirlwind-romance kind of thing."

She bit her lip to keep the joy bubbling up inside from bursting out. "A definite whirlwind. More like a tornado."

He grinned. "We didn't have a chance for the whole dinner-and-movies kind of thing…"

"Yeah, with the car chases, barn catching fire and all that…" She repressed a shudder at the memories, refusing to let them intrude on the moment.

"But when I looked into your eyes, I knew."

She remembered the moment she'd first met his gaze. She'd never seen eyes so green.

"Like with your parents, when you know it's right, it's right." An anxious light entered his eyes, lighting the emerald depths. "And we're right together, don't you think?"

"I do think so," she whispered past the lump in her throat.

Relief flooded his face and love shone bright in his gaze. "Alicia, will you marry me?"

Overflowing with happiness, she slipped to her knees and wrapped her arms around him. "Yes!"

"Yes!" Charlie repeated and jumped from the couch to hug them both.

EPILOGUE

Four weeks later and they were no closer to finding Jake. Leo had to fight to keep the hope that they would rescue him from fizzling out.

The team was working around the clock hunting down leads on their missing coworker and friend. So far nothing had panned out. The more time that went by, the more Leo despaired for his friend's life.

And their case against Reginald Dupree was teetering because their lead witness, Esme Durpee, who had been living under an assumed name in Witness Protection, had gone missing. She'd written a note saying she'd left of her own accord and didn't want to be responsible for anyone else getting hurt because of her.

Two women had died because they resembled her. The other two missing women had been found, alive but traumatized, in a hunter's cabin in the woods north of Settler's Valley.

Losing Esme was a huge blow.

Now the team needed to find her, to not only have her testify against her brother but to keep her safe from Angus Dupree.

But tonight was a rare respite from the turmoil. "Burgers are ready," called Thomas Battali, the K-9 unit's head trainer. He and his wife, Sandy, had graciously opened their home for a backyard picnic for the team.

Sandy handed plates to Leo, Ian and Max. Ian and Max headed for the food.

Leo searched the brightly lit patio for his soon-to-be bride and found her near the fire pit. Alicia sparkled. Her dark hair was loose about her shoulders and her face beamed as she laughed with agents Harper Prentiss and Nina Atkins, dog trainer extraordinaire Faith Rand and the team's general assistant, Christy Burton.

Leo was glad to see she was making friends with the ladies of the unit. He had hoped she'd find moving to Billings agreeable.

The Howard ranch had sold quickly and the horses were now settled in their new home, allowing Harmon to move into his new digs at a swanky retirement center, where he was learning to golf. Alicia had rented a small apartment for the next few months for her and Charlie. Leo had given notice on his studio apartment and they were searching for a house that would provide a stable and loving place for their new family.

Alicia glanced in Leo's direction as the ladies moved toward the barbecue. The love shining in her eyes touched his heart. She pointed to where Tim Ramsey entertained Charlie with a horseback ride on his shoulders. His little-boy giggles filled the backyard. Leo grinned, appreciating that the team had so easily and readily accepted Alicia and Charlie into the inner circle.

If only Jake was here.

Dylan and Julianne came out of the house and joined Leo.

"You getting in line?" Dylan asked, gesturing toward the food table where Ian and Max were already filling their plates.

"After you," Leo said and fell into step with the team's computer whiz. "Though I never expected I'd be getting married before you. How's Zara faring at the academy?"

"Things are still iffy," Dylan said. "She's not sure they will graduate on time."

"Any idea what's going on?"

"None. It's all hush-hush. And frustrating."

Leo didn't envy Dylan and Zara's situation. After all they'd gone through, they deserved to have their happy ending.

Julianne linked her arm through Leo's. "I'm so excited for you and Alicia."

"Thank you," he replied. "I hear you're going to be one of Zara's bridesmaids."

"That I am," she said, her voice taking on a wistful tone. "It's the closest I'll ever get to the altar and a groom." She slipped away to join the other ladies in line.

Leo had to wonder what was in her past to prompt her comment. Something she never talked about. He knew there was a story there.

As he surveyed those gathered around, he mused that everyone had a story. Some more dramatic and traumatic than others. But the respect among the agents, trainers and staff rose above any one person's past.

His gaze strayed to Alicia. He was filled with wonder at the new story he now had with a beautiful woman and an adorable son. His heart had been made whole by love. Where once there had been loneliness and guilt, now there was a certainty of hope and happiness. He could handle whatever life threw at him with Alicia and Charlie by his side, and faith that God would see them through.

* * * * *

If you enjoyed GUARDIAN by Terri Reed, look for the other books in the CLASSIFIED K-9 UNIT miniseries:

SHERIFF by Laura Scott
SPECIAL AGENT by Valerie Hansen
BOUNTY HUNTER by Lynette Eason
BODYGUARD by Shirlee McCoy
TRACKER by Lenora Worth
CLASSIFIED K-9 UNIT CHRISTMAS
by Terri Reed and Lenora Worth

Dear Reader,

Writing about K-9 officers and their handlers is always a pleasure. True was a heroic dog and learning about water search-and-rescue was fascinating. I'm always amazed and impressed by the abilities of canines.

FBI agent Leo Gallagher, True's human partner, overcame a traumatic past to become a hero. So often we humans let our past define us just as Leo had done, but with the help and love of the right woman for him, he was able to look to the future with hope.

For widow Alicia Duncan, trust didn't come easy after the hurt and betrayal of her late husband. For her son's sake, she chose not to let bitterness take root, which allowed her to be open to finding love again with a man of integrity and honor.

I hope you've enjoyed the first book in the new Love Inspired Suspense continuity series. If you'd like to see Zara and Dylan's story, look online for *Agent-in-Training*. And keep an eye out for the next five installments in the series to see how the men and woman of the FBI Tactical K-9 Unit rescue Jake and take down the Duprees.

Until we meet again, may God bless you and keep you in His care,

Get 2 Free Books,

Plus 2 Free Gifts—

just for trying the Reader Service!

*The search for a missing colleague puts an FBI agent
right in the path of a prison break...and her
ex-boyfriend.*

*Read on for an excerpt from
SHERIFF,
the next book in the exciting new series
CLASSIFIED K-9 UNIT.*

The low rumble of a car engine caused FBI agent Julianne Martinez to freeze in her tracks. She quickly gave her K-9 partner, Thunder, the hand signal for "stay." The Big Thicket region of east Texas was densely covered with trees and brush. This particular area of the woods had also been oddly silent.

Until now.

Moving silently, she angled toward the road, sucking in a harsh breath when she caught a glimpse of a black-and-white prison van.

The van abruptly stopped with enough force that it rocked back and forth. Frowning, she edged closer to get a better look.

There was a black SUV sitting diagonally across the road, barricading the way.

Julianne rushed forward. As she pulled out her weapon, she heard a bang and a crash followed by a man tumbling out of the back of the prison van. The large bald guy dressed in prison orange made a beeline toward the SUV.

Another man stood in the center of the road pointing a weapon at the van driver.

A prison break!

"Stop!" Julianne pulled her weapon and shot at the gunman. Her aim was true, and the gunman flinched, staggering backward, but didn't go down.

He had to be wearing body armor.

The gunman shot the driver through the windshield, then came running directly at Julianne.

She ducked behind a tree, then took a steadying breath. Julianne eased from one tree to the next as Thunder watched, waiting for her signal.

Crack!

She ducked, feeling the whiz of the bullet as it missed her by a fraction of an inch.

After a long moment, she was about to risk another glance when the gunman popped out from behind a tree.

"Stop right there," he shouted. "Put your hands in the air."

Angry that she hadn't anticipated the gunman's move, Julianne held his gaze.

"Put your hands in the air!" he repeated harshly.

"Fire that gun and I'll plant a bullet between your eyes," a familiar deep husky Texan drawl came from out of nowhere.

Brody Kenner?

Don't miss
SHERIFF by Laura Scott,
available wherever
Love Inspired® Suspense ebooks are sold.

www.LoveInspired.com

Turn your love of reading into rewards you'll love with
Harlequin My Rewards

**Join for FREE today at
www.HarlequinMyRewards.com**

Earn **FREE BOOKS** of your choice.

Experience **EXCLUSIVE OFFERS** and contests.

Enjoy **BOOK RECOMMENDATIONS**
selected just for you.

PLUS! Sign up now
and get **500** points
right away!

Earn **FREE REWARDS**
Join Today!
HarlequinMyRewards.com

MYR16R